M000266816

AWAY FROM KEYBOARD COLLECTION

BY LETHAL
FORCE

PATRICIA D. EDDY

If you love sexy vampires and demons, I'd love to send you the prequel to the upcoming Immortal Protectors series. FOR FREE! Sign up for my Unstoppable Newsletter on my website and tell me where to send your free book! http://patriciadeddy.com.

PROLOGUE

Twenty Years Ago

Joey

THAT LAST COSMO WAS A MISTAKE. As I follow Uma and Belle into our third bar of the night, my stomach lurches. After today, I'm never drinking again.

"Our table's in the back," Uma shouts over Queen blasting from the sound system. "We have the karaoke stage from seven to eight."

"I am *not* singing," I protest. "I love you, babe, but—" I belch, tasting bile, and groan, "—karaoke is the one line I will never cross."

The three of us perch on stools around the high-top table, and Uma checks her watch. "Betty and Pilar should be here soon, and they'll drag your pre-med ass up there."

"They'll fail." A server swings by with water, and I down half the glass, praying it'll be enough to stop me from hurling all over my "I'm with the bride" t-shirt. "I'll do anything for you. But I won't do that." My voice warbles in a pitiful attempt at mimicking MeatLoaf's iconic song, and my two best friends applaud as I take a half bow and barely manage not to fall off my stool.

And that's when I see him.

For a few seconds, I'm stone cold sober. Staring at the profile of the man who slipped a ring on my finger six months ago and promised me as soon as I finished med school, we'd get married.

Except...he's supposed to be halfway around the world. Deployed with the Marine Corps. Instead, he's sitting thirty feet away, staring into his beer, while a scantily clad bar-bunny presses her ass against his hip.

"Oh, *hell* no," I say as I bounce off the stool and weave my way through the crowds. Uma calls my name, but I'm too angry. Too focused on Ford to respond to her.

As I reach the little floozie sucking a neon green drink through a bright pink straw, I narrow my eyes, and she makes a little *o* with her perfectly painted lips. Ford doesn't notice her scampering away, but when I clear my throat and say his name, he flinches, his shoulders slumping further before he slowly turns to face me.

"Want to tell me what my fiancé is doing in San Diego? In a bar? With...*that*? I jerk my head towards the bar-bunny, who's now grinding her hips against another Marine in dress whites.

He doesn't speak for several long seconds, his mouth slack, defeat marring his features.

"Well?"

"I...we...it's a three-day furlough. Just enough time to—"

"To cheat on me?"

Ford pushes his glass away and reaches for me. "Joey—"

"Don't 'Joey' me. You're in a bar, in our home town, and you didn't call the woman you're supposed to marry. Tell me what else I'm supposed to think?" My voice cracks as I try to make myself heard over the music, and I slap my hand over my mouth as my stomach lurches again. Shit. I'm going to be sick. Everything I thought I knew... I can't do this now. Can't watch him try to come up with excuses that'll make this all okay. It'll never be okay.

"I thought you were one of the good ones." I pull and twist until the ring pops off my finger, then slam it down on the bar next to his beer. "Go fuck yourself, Ford."

Whirling, I almost go down, but Uma and Belle appear behind me, each taking an arm. "Ford?" Uma asks as her gaze bounces between me and my now-former fiancé.

"I have to get out of here," I say, my voice choked with the tears I won't let fall in front of him. Pushing out of my best friends' arms, I stumble back to the table, grab my purse, and make my way to the door.

Bursting into the cool evening air, I start to run for Market Street. I can catch a cab there to take me home, and all I want right now is to throw up and cry.

"Joey!" Ford's voice behind me propels my feet faster, but I can't see much through the tears welling in my eyes. "Joey, wait, please!"

He catches up to me on the corner, steps in front of me, and wraps me in his arms. The tender gesture shatters me, and I dissolve into hoarse, choking sobs. "You...bastard. I hate you."

"Call me any name you want, buttercup. I deserve them all. But," he dips his head so his lips are close to my ear, "I swear on my life I didn't cheat on you. I would never. You're...you're it for me."

As a tear lands on my bare shoulder, I peer up at him. In the two years we've been together, I've never seen him so...unsure. "Then why—?"

"Can we go somewhere? Your place? Mine? Anywhere you want. Just to talk?" He presses my ring into my palm, and a fresh wave of tears tumbles down my cheeks. "Please, baby. I can't lose you. I love you. I'd die before I'd cheat on you."

"Lisa's at my apartment. With her boyfriend." I sniffle and swipe my hands over my cheeks. "I told her I wouldn't be back tonight."

"Then my place. Please?" Emotion thickens his tone, and he feels so good, smells so good, and he's so earnest...I give in.

"Okay. But you're paying for my cab when you're done *explaining*."

Ford nods, drapes his arm around my shoulder, and steers me down the sidewalk. His tiny studio is only a few blocks from here, and we walk, not saying a word, as my mind races. He's the most honest man I've ever met. I'm pretty sure there's a picture of him next to the dictionary definition of boy scout. So if he says he didn't cheat, he didn't.

But that doesn't let him off the hook.

—————

As soon as he closes his apartment door, he heads for the fridge for two bottles of water. "Want one?"

"I want an explanation." But, I'm still a little tipsy, so I take the water and rest my back against the door.

"I don't know...fuck. They warned us about this." He stalks over to his little window. The view isn't anything—just a little courtyard with a decrepit fountain, but he's fixated on it like it's a lifeline. "The first time you kill someone. It's...I can't...you don't deserve this darkness."

Ford braces his forearm on the upper windowsill. He barely fits in this apartment. Six-foot-ten, not bulky, but hard as a rock, he's always been my granite teddy bear. The nicest, sweetest man in the entire world. But now, he's so distant. I approach carefully, and when I rest my hand on his back, he stiffens. "Don't."

"Don't what? Touch you? Ford? We're...I love you."

"I don't deserve you. Your love. Not after what I've done."

My hackles go up, and I back off a couple of steps towards the door. "You said you didn't cheat—"

"I didn't!" He whirls, and I see the truth in his eyes. He didn't. But he didn't just kill one person. He killed a lot of them.

"You went to war, Marine. You had to know it'd be bad."

"Not this bad. They gave us the furlough so we could get our heads on straight. Hell, my CO *told* me to find you and bury all this balls-deep—fuck. I'm sorry, baby."

"I like you balls-deep in me."

This makes him laugh, but it's not his normal, relaxed chuckle. No, this sounds like he's forcing the sound through a steel trap. Given how quickly one of the muscles in his jaw is ticking, that's probably pretty accurate.

"Stay with me tonight, Joey. Please. I don't care if we do anything but sleep. Just...stay."

Linking our fingers, I lead him to the bed. He's putty in my hands. So far from the commanding, strong, confident man who left me for his first oversees deployment six months ago. He lets me undress him, staring off into the corner like it holds the answers to the secrets of the universe. When I'm down to my tank and panties and he's only wearing briefs, we snuggle under the blanket. "You can talk to me, Ford. Whatever it is...I'll still love you."

But he stays silent, and as I drift off to the sleep, I wonder if he'll ever come back to me.

———

THE NEXT MORNING, I open my eyes before the sun comes up. Ford still sleeps soundly, though his face is anything but relaxed. I don't want to wake him, but I have study group in three hours, and I need a shower and...clothes that don't make me look like that bar-bunny from last night. Grabbing my skirt, I pad over to his kitchenette counter and find a little notebook and a pen.

Ford, I love you. I don't know what happened over there or why you can't tell me about it. But love requires trust. And hard work. I know you leave this afternoon, but please...think about what I said. We'll never survive if you can't let me share your pain. -Joey

After I slip on my heels and my too-short skirt—I'm going to freeze trying to catch a cab this time of the morning—I escape out the door and head for home.

"ASSHOLE," I mutter as the third cab passes me by. I guess my bachelorette party attire doesn't make for a guaranteed fare. My apartment is only another ten blocks away, but my feet already ache, and my arms are two skinny icicles covered with goose-bumps. I turn down an alley as a shortcut, but three steps out onto the next street, a muffled scream and a thump sends fear snaking frigid tendrils around my heart.

Picking up the pace, I focus on the four lane road only a couple blocks away. Traffic streams by at high speed this time of the morning, and there, I'll find people.

"Two-for-one?"

The raspy voice startles me only a second before a hand claps over my mouth and I'm dragged into the shadows of a large, darkened building. Flailing my legs, I catch a second man in the stomach with the heel of my shoe, and he mutters something in Spanish.

My screams go nowhere, and once the second man recovers and glances down at his shirt, where I've left a rip and a bloody scratch, his dark eyes turn almost black. "You'll pay for that, bitch."

Clawing at the strong arm banded around my waist, I draw more blood. The scents of cigarettes and bad aftershave surround me. The second man pulls a pouch from his back pocket as the first man propels me towards a black van.

If they get me in there, I'm dead.

Throwing my head back, I feel a satisfying crunch as I hit the first man's nose and smell blood. The hand slips from my mouth as he cries out, and I scream with everything in me. But he still has me around the waist, and I can't escape his hold.

"She broke my nose!"

And then I'm flying, my head hitting the van, sending me crumpling to the ground. *Get up, Joey. Get up, now.*

When the dark haze clears from my vision, the two of them stand over me. "Wrong place, wrong time, honey." The flash of a needle paralyzes me for a second too long, and by the time I lurch to my feet, they're ready for me.

Broken nose guy grabs my wrist and twists my arm behind my back as he slams me face-first into the side of the van. The prick in my arm barely stings, and I scream for help again, but it's fainter than I intend.

Oh God.

My limbs start to feel heavy, and the men's hands rove over my body. Slaps to my ass. Rough fingers on my inner thighs. And I can't fight. My eyelids weigh ten pounds each, and I fight to keep them open.

But it's no use. The van door makes an odd metallic screech, and then I land on something soft and lumpy. With a moan, I let my eyes close as I realize what I'm lying on.

Another unconscious woman.

Panic seizes my heart in a vise, and I struggle to breathe as the drugs pull me under. I can't move, can't scream, and as the van door slams shut and I drift off, I think of Ford, and how I might never see him again.

THE SOUND of whimpering rouses me enough to force my eyes open—and then wish I hadn't.

A harsh light illuminates expanses of skin—white, brown, golden... There have to be at least ten girls in here with me, all dressed in short skirts, strappy tanks, or nothing but bras and panties.

Oh God.

Three of them huddle in a corner, holding on to one another. The rest sit alone, some crying, others looking shell-shocked. I push up on an elbow, and then the stench hits me. It smells like the worst public bathroom on the planet in here. Hot, muggy, and still, the air chokes me, and I retch, the space spinning around me until my head hits the floor.

Trembling fingers touch my arm, and I jerk away.

"Shhh. I won't hurt you. I'm Emmie. You'll be dizzy for a little while," she whispers. "But try not to throw up. The only place for it is the bucket over there, and they only come to empty it once a day."

"Once...a...day?" I don't understand. Anything. "Where are we? What's going on?" Each word sends pain pulsing through my skull, and I dig my knuckles into my temples to try to stop the pounding.

Blinking away the tears gathering in my eyes, I try to focus on Emmie. Greasy brown hair hangs from a haggard face. Dark circles brace her eyes, and her lower lip is swollen and red, like she's been chewing on it nonstop.

"They are going to sell us."

"No. They can't...we're...Americans—"

Another voice, this one harsh, echoes on the metal walls, "You think that makes a damn bit of difference?"

"Quiet, Hannah! Or they'll come," Emmie hisses at the second girl.

"Fuck 'em," Hannah spits back.

A loud metal sound shakes the walls, and all of the girls tense, shrinking away as doors open wide at the end of the long, narrow room. More light spills in, and I think I can make out the vaguely corrugated walls of a railcar. Three men fill the opening, one holding a baseball bat, the other with what looks like a gun, but thicker.

Emmie drags me back against the wall with her. I can't look away from the center man's face. His brown eyes hold no warmth, and a long scar bisects his cheek. "New girls, stand up." Pulling driver's licenses from his pocket, he says, "Rachel Mendoza and Josephine Taylor."

"You have to," Emmie whispers in my ear. "Or they'll hurt all of us."

I don't know if my legs will hold me, but I try, crash to my knees, and then finally wobble to standing. Across the railcar, another woman—a girl, really—jerks up with a curse. "You won't fucking get away with this," she says in a heavily accented voice.

The man stalks over to her and backhands her hard enough to send her careening into the wall with a yelp. "You will address me as Jefe. Until you reach the auction, I own you."

I'm too terrified to speak, and when he approaches me, I press my back into the wall, staring down at the shiny alligator pattern and metal tips on his shoes. "Pretty little thing. Older, I think. How old are you, *chica*? Twenty?"

"Twenty-two," I whisper.

He grabs my chin, turning my head this way and that. "Open your mouth."

The demand shocks me, and I don't think before saying, "What?"

Thick fingers wrap around my throat, cutting off my air, and his dead eyes bore into me. "You get one warning, bitch. Do as you are told, never speak without addressing me properly, and you will not be punished. Otherwise..." He lets the threat hang between us until the edges of my vision darken, and then releases me.

As I suck in lungfuls of the disgusting, thick air, he repeats his order. "Open your mouth."

This time, I obey, and he pulls my jaw down as far as it will go. "Good teeth." I don't have time to process why he cares about my teeth before he yanks up my tank and palms one of my breasts, pinching the nipple hard enough to make me cry out. "Perky tits. Small."

"Get your hands off me, you bastard!"

"*Estupida, pequeña perra.* I was being nice," he snarls. Wrapping his hand in my long, blond hair, he yanks me forward and drags me to the very center of the railcar. With a kick to the back of my legs, he sends me to my hands and knees. "Do not move."

Oh, hell no.

I'm almost to my feet when he slugs me across the cheek. The impact sends me whirling to my left, and unable to keep my feet under me, I fall to the ground, my head slamming into metal. The coppery taste of blood fills my mouth, and I spit and whimper as his hand tightens on the back of my neck.

"I would have made your first time private," he says as he kneels next to me. "But you have earned your first punishment."

When he reaches under my skirt and rips off my panties, I scream.

FIVE DAYS. I've been trapped here for five days. I think. Time stretches out in endless minutes, all blending together. The stench. The sobs of the girls around me. The indignity of having to pee—and poop—in a bucket in front of everyone.

We sleep curled on the floor as far away from that corner as we can. Two more girls have joined us, and every so often, *Jefe* or his goons come in with candy bars and bottled water. If we want to eat and drink...we have to let them...do what they want with us.

I've lost count of how many times and ways I've been violated. Emmie doesn't talk anymore. Hannah lost all her fight the third time one of the bigger guys forced her to suck him off.

Huddled in the corner as far from the door as I can, I cradle my left hand. *Jefe* ripped my engagement ring off as soon as he was done raping me for the first time, and broke my finger in the process. I set it and had Emmie tear strips from my tank and break the heel off my shoe to use as a splint.

We don't have names here. Not to *Jefe*. Numbers only. He only calls me Twelve. Before Emmie—Seven to *Jefe*—stopped responding to me, I asked her if she worried we'd eventually forget who we used to be. But she didn't answer me.

I don't want to forget. "I'm Joey Taylor," I whisper. "I'm going to be a doctor. I'm going to help people."

A sob catches in my throat as I realize I'm probably lying to myself. *Jefe* burned our driver's licenses in front of us. The other girls...half of them lived on the streets before they were taken. No one will miss them.

Eventually, someone will look for me. But how long will it take? Ford's in Iraq. Probably doesn't even know I'm gone. I told Uma I had clinicals this week. She won't expect to hear much from me. Belle was headed off for a vacation with her folks right after the party. But Pilar's wedding is in a week. When I don't show up for that...

I start to cry. Odd. I didn't think I had any tears left in me.

A loud crash followed by gunfire makes us all scream and scramble together in the corner. Footsteps pound, we hear shouts, and then *Jefe* bursts through the doors, heads right for us, and grabs me by the hair. He hauls me against him, a gun pressed to my temple.

"Put the weapon down and let the girl go," a man wearing an FBI vest says from the door.

"No fucking chance," *Jefe* growls. "You let me walk out of here, alive, or I'll put a bullet through her brain."

Do it.

I don't know where that thought comes from. I want to live. Except...everything hurts. And...after what they've done to me...

Two more officers flank the first, and *Jefe* slams the barrel into my cheek. "I mean it! I'll do it!"

One of the FBI agents...he almost looks a little like Ford. Sandy hair. Kind eyes. I don't want it to end like this. With me broken, bruised, and well on my way to losing myself completely.

I make a fist, squeeze my eyes shut, and then slam my fist into *Jefe's* balls. As soon as his hold on my neck loosens, I drop down onto the floor.

Five shots. And then *Jefe* falls on top of me, his blood soaking into my dirty tank, dripping onto my matted hair, my eyes, even filling my ears. I can't breathe, and when the heavy weight of his body is suddenly lifted off of me and those kind eyes meet mine, I start to scream.

Ford

As our transport rolls up to the base, I shove the creased note back into a plastic bag and tuck it in my front pocket. I don't know how many times I've read it. A hundred? More?

We'll never survive if you can't let me share your pain.

She's right. But when I close my eyes at night, all I see is that market the suicide bomber blew up. And those kids three days later. Dying. From our bullets. It doesn't matter that the insurgents were using them as shields. Or that we got the guys responsible for the bombs that killed more than a hundred Kuwaiti women and children.

I'll always know...I was one of the pieces of shit who killed them.

"Thank God," Jessup says as the transpo slows to a stop and he jumps out. "Lawton can finally send a fucking message to his girl."

"Shut up," I snap. "You didn't see her face that night, asshole."

"Didn't need to. You've described it in perfect detail a hundred times." He ducks out of the way as I throw a punch at his shoulder. "You were in a shitty mood the whole mission. Five and a half weeks of watching you fold and unfold that note. How the hell she's willing to marry a sappy fuck like you, I have no idea."

Neither do I. Following Jessup into the barracks, I dump my rucksack on my bunks and start unpacking. The mail room across the yard looms, despite not being able to see it through the walls of the tent.

"Well? What are you waiting for?" Jessup asks.

"If I call her, she'll want to know what happened." I snag one of my spare boots and start polishing it. I can already see my face in the damn thing. But it's been covered in blood more times than not in the past year, and every time I put them on, I see it. Smell it. "Once she finds out, she'll never look at me the same way again."

"What does she think happens in war, man?" Brasher asks

as he lays a towel out on the floor and starts to break down his weapon. "People die."

"She's twenty-two," I say. "She still looks at the world like it's all shiny and new. Fuck, she's in med school to *make a difference*. And she will. That girl's going to save lives—over and over again. I can't ask her to come home to a killer."

I run a hand over the fuzz on my head. When we're in-country, we all get a little lazy with the razor. Jessup stoops so he's right in my face. "I don't like pulling rank, Lawton. But if you don't get your head out of your ass, I'm telling the Staff Sergeant that you need to be put on leave. We're headed back out there in five days, and if you're not 100%, then you don't deserve to stand at my side. Call the girl or consider yourself unfit to serve."

AN HOUR LATER, I hold an ice pack to my jaw and hover at the door to the mail room. "Got anything for Lawton?"

The letter's thin, and the handwriting on the outside...it's not Joey's, and there's no return address.

Tearing into the envelope before I even move away from the counter, I pull out the single sheet of paper.

Dear Ford,

I don't know how to tell you this. I can't say the words. I tried to call, but I couldn't. But writing them isn't any easier. When I left your apartment...I never made it home.

He...they had me for a week. So many bad things happened. Things I don't want to think about. Fifteen of us. Trapped in a rail-car. We were supposed to be sold. But the FBI found us.

I'm alive. In the hospital. My sister says this isn't a dream, but I don't believe her. I'm sorry you had to find out like this. But I didn't want you to call and wonder why I didn't answer.

Joey

Stumbling out into the hot desert night, I barely make it to the phones before I see red. Someone hurt her. Someone violated her. Was going to *sell* her. The date on the letter...it's a month ago. She sent this a month ago and didn't hear anything back from me.

Static crackles over the line as it rings, and I don't understand why she's not answering. As I'm about to disconnect, there's a click, and a tentative "Hello?"

"Who's this?" I demand.

"Who's *this?*" Now the woman's pissed.

Get it together, asshole. It's probably her roommate. "Ford. I'm Joey's fiancé. Is she there?"

The woman sighs. "This is Lisa. She said you'd call. Thought it would have been at least three weeks ago, though. You're a jerk, you know that?"

Anger stiffens my spine, and my knuckles crack as my fingers tighten on the receiver. "Listen, I already feel like shit. But I just got back from a long deployment—no communications in or out. Are you going to let me talk to her?"

"Really? You didn't know...?"

"Of course not! You think I would have abandoned her? Never. I love her."

Another sigh, and Lisa curses under her breath. "Ford, she left. I came home a few days ago, her stuff was gone, and there was a note on the counter. All it said was 'I have to go away for a while. Here's the rent for last three months of the lease.' No forwarding address, no nothing."

"What? I don't understand. She had to say more than *that.*"

"She hasn't said much of anything since it happened. Look, I wish I could help. We weren't close, but she was nice, and she didn't deserve what they did to her. If she calls, I'll tell her you were out of contact until today. But all I can tell you to do is contact her sister."

Mumbling a weak "thank you," I hang up and sink down

onto the floor, my head in my hands. What if I've lost her for good? Shit. She was right. I didn't trust her with my pain, and now we might be done for.

———

FOUR DAYS LATER, I'm back in San Diego, knocking on her sister's door. Gerry's face hardens when she peers out at me through the gap in the chain. "You have some nerve."

As she starts to shut the door, I wedge my foot in the gap. "Within an hour of getting Joey's letter, I was in my CO's office begging for the next flight back to the States. I've been deployed on a mission for more than five weeks. I *never* would have abandoned her. I love her. Please, tell me where she is. I have to explain why I didn't come when she needed me."

Gerry's eyes soften, and she presses her lips together as she nods. Withdrawing my foot, I wait for her to close the door a bit and unhook the chain. Ten years older than Joey, she could be her twin, if not for the slight lines around her eyes and the much darker hair.

"Come on in, Ford. We need to have a little chat."

———

I LURCH BACK to my apartment, the bottle of bourbon half empty and dangling from my fingers. Joey took a leave of absence from med school. When she moved out of her apartment, she wouldn't give her sister her new address. She won't talk to anyone—not her family, not her friends, and certainly not me. Not even when her sister called her and started to explain where I'd been.

"He didn't know—"

"I can't do this, Gerry. I just...can't."

Her voice sounded so weak. Afraid. And I don't know what

to do besides down another healthy gulp of bourbon and fall, face-first, into my bed.

Over the next month, I write her letter after letter. Gerry promised to deliver them. And every one comes back *Return to Sender.*

I've lost her. And what's worse? All her pain, all her suffering...it's on me. Because I couldn't let her in.

1
_____

Present Day

Joey

A HINT of a breeze stirs the flap on the tent door, and I sink down onto the cot, take off my sneakers, and rub my sore feet. "I'm getting too old for this shit," I mutter. At forty-two, my joints don't recover like they used to, and I miss my bed with its thick mattress and weighted blanket.

The buzz of the generator drones from the other side of the canvas wall, and Ivy flounces in, all twenty-one-years of boundless energy and optimism. The light in her eyes...I used to have that.

"Does this country ever cool down?" she asks as she strips off her t-shirt. Standing in front of the fan in a sports bra and her dark blue pants, she holds out her arms, sweat glistening on the tops of her rather large breasts.

Rolling my eyes, I sink back onto the thin pillow and pull

the sheet up to my chest. "Get some sleep. We have an eight-hour drive tomorrow. Where's Mia?"

"She's chatting up Dr. Phillips. I think the two of them are a thing now."

I don't have the energy to roll my eyes again, so I close them and hope the third female member of our little team doesn't make too much noise when she wanders in sometime around three in the morning.

"How do you sleep when it's this hot?" Ivy asks.

"You learn." I shouldn't be so snippy with her. It's not her fault Turkmenistan is in the middle of a heat wave. Or that she happened to sign up for a tour just as Doctors Without Borders was planning their first trip here in more than ten years. I crack one eye open to find her half-naked. "Put some clothes on, Ivy. We have to respect our host country's culture."

"But—"

Holding up my hand, I press my lips together for a moment to stop myself from saying something I'll regret. She's a good kid and a hard worker. But these conditions aren't for everyone. "When we travel to other countries, we have to do our best to fit in. Otherwise, we might not be allowed back. Think of all the kids we vaccinated today. None of them would be protected. Cholera is one of the primary killers of children in Turk-menistan. Sixty kids. No, sixty-three." I do the math in my head, and her eyes widen. "Sixty-three kids *today* who won't die from a preventable disease. By the end of the week when we're closer to Turkmenabat, our numbers will be close to a thousand."

Ivy grabs her long-sleeved scrubs top and pulls it over her head. Her pants go back on next. "I'm sorry, Dr. Taylor. You're right."

"Joey." I sink back down and roll over. "As for how to sleep? Put on fresh socks. You'd be amazed how much cooler your feet feel."

As Ivy rustles about across the tent, I reach for the chain around my neck, pulling the ring from its hiding place between my breasts. I've worn it around my neck every day for twenty years, and it's become my touchstone. It'll be dark soon. I don't like the dark. Haven't ever since...

When I close my eyes at night, I see the faces of the men who ruined me. Until I reach for my ring. And then...sometimes...I can see the man I used to love. The man I ran away from because I was too scared, too damaged, too afraid.

Tonight, I try to call up a good memory. Happier times. Before I ruined everything.

"Joey, trust me," Ford says as he holds out his hand.

"You do know gravity's a thing, right?" Staring down at the amusement park spread out before us, I then turn my gaze to the zipline. "That little thing is going to support both of us? I don't think so."

"Buttercup, I'll hold you the whole way down. And...I'm pretty sure I saw an extra large box of Red Vines for sale at the concession stand by the ferris wheel. One trip, and the candy's on me." His deep voice rumbles against my chest as he wraps his arm around me. We're already harnessed together, and the line behind us starts to get restless.

This was my idea. A stupid one, I can see now, but still...my idea. Something to help me get over my fear of heights. Plus, Ford swears it's fun.

Throwing my arms around his neck, I bury my face against his soft t-shirt. "I'm not watching."

As he steps off the platform, he cups my cheek and guides my lips to his. Suddenly, we're flying, and the heat of his kiss, the way his arousal presses into my stomach as we glide five hundred feet, the wind ruffling my hair...it's like nothing I've ever felt before. It's...perfection.

There's a small thud and a muffled curse back in the tent,

and the memory fades. My hand moves to my pocket, and I find the paperclip I always keep there. Working it free, I drag it across my stomach. Not hard enough to make me bleed. Just hard enough to make me feel. Something. Anything but the paralyzing regrets and fears I carry with me every single day.

The tingling sensation calms me, and the slight pain as I press the tip in a little harder, just in one spot—lets the tension seep from my limbs. It's enough. For tonight, I'll be able to sleep for an hour at a time—maybe even two—before the nightmares come.

THE NEXT DAY dawns even hotter than the last, and before I do much more than brush my teeth and put on the white vest that marks me as one of the doctors, sweat is dripping down my back. But even though this isn't our official camp—the locals are lining up, waiting for us. Turkmenistan has been without advanced medical care in the rural parts of the country for more than ten years, and while many still distrust us—our little group of six is made up of two Americans, three Brits, and Mia, who's French—they're desperate for mobile medicine.

I grab my clipboard and head for the triage line. *"Adyň näme?"* I ask in Turkmen as I kneel in front of a boy no older than six. It's one of the only phrases I know, but it works with the little kids.

"Batyr," he says softly with a smile.

"Hi, Batyr. *Meniň adym* Dr. Joey."

He shrinks behind his mother as one of our security guys— and our translator—helps me explain what happens next. The brief exam, the cholera vaccine, and any potential side effects over the next few days. Six boys, three girls, and four adults later, a hand on my shoulder makes me jerk and whirl around.

"Shit, Ray. Don't *do* that."

Dr. Raymond Phillips, the senior physician in charge, passes me a bottle of water from the case in the corner of the tent. "Sorry, Joey. But if we don't start out for Turkmenabat soon, we won't make it before nightfall."

Glancing back at the intake line, I do the math in my head. "If you let me keep working while the crew packs up the sleeping tents, I can finish up with these last six patients in thirty minutes."

"Joey—"

"Please. These people *need* us. The last mother and baby I saw walked for two days to get here. There aren't many left. I'll make dinner when we get there."

"You mean you'll pass out the MREs?" He chuckles and shakes his head. "Fine. But make sure I get the shepherd's pie one. None of that chicken casserole shite."

I blow out a breath as I twist the cap off my water bottle. "Shepherd's pie it is. Thanks."

WE DON'T MAKE it to Turkmenabat before dark. Two flat tires and a faulty headlight force us to stop a hundred kilometers from our destination. The locals we hired to drive us argue quietly in Turkmen as they help set up two of the small tents a short distance from the road, and I collapse face first on top of the sleeping bag, not even bothering to take off my shoes.

The first shot banishes sleep instantly, and I'm on my feet, my heart in my throat. Ivy screams, and I grab her and slap my hand over her mouth, then drag her to the back corner of the tent. Mia joins us, and we huddle together, shaking. Shouts and more gunfire surround us, and I start chanting silently, *"Not again. Please...not again."*

"What do you want?" Dr. Phillips says, his tone devoid of the authority it usually carries. His fear ratchets up my own, and I squeeze my hands hard enough to leave little crescent-shaped indentations in my palms.

The tent flap opens as a single shot pierces the night, and behind a man clad all in brown holding an AK-47, Dr. Phillips crumples to the ground, blood streaming from his head, his eyes open and fixed on me.

No. Ray. We're dead. We're all dead.

"You. Up," the man with the gun says, gesturing at me. "Now."

I can't move. Mia and Ivy tremble on either side of me. The scent of blood fills my nose, and my vision wavers as the man strides forward, grabs my arm, and yanks me to my feet.

"Please!" I cry. "Don't hurt us! We're doctors! We just want to help!"

He propels me out of the tent where four other men—each holding one of the massive guns—wait. One of them takes the flaps of my white vest and rips them open, spinning me around and jerking it down my arms before tossing it away. A second man approaches with a bunch of dark blue fabric clutched in his massive hands, and he throws something at me. "Put this on or we do it for you."

No, no, no.... I can hear *Jefe's* voice in my head as he forces me to the ground in that railcar all those years ago, and my inability to move in the present earns me a smack to the face.

"Now!"

Ivy and Mia are dragged from the tent behind me, still holding on to one another. The men whisper amongst themselves, gesturing to them as I pull the dark abaya over my head. It hides my body from my neck to my feet, the sleeves easily four inches too long.

Our attackers pull two more abayas from a duffel bag and thrust them at Ivy and Mia. The girls look to me, and I wish I could offer them some sort of comfort. But I can't. "Do what they say."

One by one, they grab our hands and secure our wrists in front of us with duct tape, then tug the sleeves of our abayas lower so no one can see the dark gray bindings. Tears stream down my cheeks, and the tallest of our attackers uses a thick strip of scratchy, black material to gag me, then covers my entire head with a full-face scarf. The *boshiya's* material is only sheer enough to see through over my eyes, and to anyone looking, I'm nothing more than a native woman in full, traditional dress. One who's unable to talk or move her arms.

They're hiding us. So no one will know we're in trouble.

Dr. Philips, Mark, one of the physician's assistants, and our two bodyguards lie dead, bullet wounds to their heads and chests leaving dark pools of blood oozing into the sandy soil.

As I'm dragged down the road away from our makeshift camp, my sobs and my heartbeat roaring in my ears obliterate all other sounds.

My thoughts race all the way to a waiting van, a good two kilometers away.

They didn't kill us. Because we're women. Because...they're going to sell us.

Panic locks my muscles, and as I'm shoved onto a bench in the back, I can do nothing but cry silently, and wonder if this time, I could find a way to die rather than endure the horrors of being brutalized yet again.

I DON'T KNOW how long we've been in this van. Sun streams through the front windshield now, high in the sky, so we've been driving for at least eight or nine hours.

Ivy and Mia are huddled together across from me. We've all stopped crying—though the occasional sob breaks through the drone of the engine. One of our captors is next to me, the other next to Ivy, and the last two in the front seats.

My bladder sends sharp pains from my stomach down my legs, my shoulders ache, and my eyes are swollen and gritty. There's no air conditioning, but the front windows are open, so at least there's a hint of a breeze. I'm covered in sweat, dehydrated, and dizzy. Ivy and Mia wriggle, apparently also desperate to relieve themselves, and whimper softly.

The man in the passenger seat says something in a language I don't understand, and the driver grunts an agreement. It's not Turkmen. I think...maybe it's Pashto, which given that we're driving south, probably means they're from Afghanistan.

A few minutes later, the van rolls to a stop, and the man at my side gets to his feet, opens the back door, and motions to me to exit.

Oh God.

So many different possibilities run through my mind as I scoot to the edge of the bench and try not to fall on my face as I climb out. Ivy and Mia follow. Full-Beard—what I've named the man—yanks my sleeves up and then cuts the tape around my wrists. He points to a stand of sad trees maybe fifty feet away. "Piss. You run, they die." No-Beard, the driver, holds a pistol to Ivy's head—at least I think that's Ivy. With their faces covered, I can't be sure. They're almost the same height.

Stumbling over the rocks and dried grasses, I make it to the trees, hike up my abaya, pull down my pants, and squat. My God, I've never felt anything so wonderful except maybe my first shower after the police rescued me from *Jefe.*

But when I get back to the road, Full-Beard tapes my wrists again before letting Ivy, then Mia visit the tree. As they usher us back towards the van, I pantomime water—or try—and Full-Beard grumbles something to No-Beard, who rummages up front and returns with three bottles.

"In the back," Full Beard says. He doesn't say another word until we're all seated again and the doors have sealed us inside.

Only then does he pull off my *boshiya*, remove my gag, and hand me the bottle. "Quick, quick, quick."

Afraid this is the only chance I'll have to drink for another half a day, I suck down the whole bottle. It's warm, but I don't care. *Please don't let me get sick,* I pray as Full-Beard slaps the empty bottle out of my bound hands, gags me again, and recovers my head. The van doesn't start moving until Ivy and Mia have had their water, and then we're bouncing down the rutted road, and I can only focus on one question.

What happens when we get to where we're going?

NOT MORE THAN AN HOUR LATER, we reach some sort of checkpoint. The van slows to a stop, and No-Beard exchanges words with someone out the driver's side window. Their voices turn angry, and next to me, Full-Beard jabs a pistol into my side. "You make a sound, you will pay."

The back doors open, and a man in a light brown uniform with a pistol strapped to his hip peers inside. "Who are they?" he asks in Turkmen, gesturing to us.

Full-Beard replies with a string of words I don't understand, and I wish the uniformed man could see my eyes. I'm pleading silently with him to realize something is off. In English, probably to reinforce just how helpless we are in this state, Full-Beard announces that we are on our way to arranged marriages with village elders near Batash. The uniformed man nods, accepting Full-Beard's words immediately, and the doors slam shut.

If they hadn't gagged us...if they hadn't forced these dark *boshiyas* over our heads...if we'd just all screamed... My tears start anew, and I dig my fingernails into my palms. I want to break the skin. To feel something besides pure terror. But then the van starts to move again, and I'm too scared to move at all.

NIGHT BRINGS PURE TERROR. I'm practically hyperventilating around the gag, and my heart feels like it's about to explode out of my chest. Or stop beating entirely. We're up in the mountains now, and it's cold. Or maybe that's just the adrenaline crash.

Ivy fell asleep against Mia a few hours ago, but I can't rest. Can't even close my eyes. If I do, I won't be able to prepare myself for anything that's coming. Full-Beard keeps leering at me, and he's gradually moved closer.

A few lights—small houses, I think, brighten the interior of the van through the windshield, and we make several turns, then stop. The barrel of a pistol presses to my side, and I yelp, which only makes Full-Beard jab me harder. "Quiet."

Nodding, I swallow my whimpers, and then they drag us out of the van and into a small, clay-walled house. We move so quickly, the rooms are a blur until a trapdoor in the floor opens, and we're shoved down a set of stairs into total darkness. But it doesn't stay dark for long. Full-Beard brings a small, bare-bulb lamp, and once he's plugged the light in, I get my first good look at our surroundings.

No windows. No other way out but the stairs. A toilet and sink in one corner. Dirty mattresses in the other. No-Beard pulls out a pocket knife. "Hands. Now."

With our bindings cut, No-Beard motions to our *boshiyas*. "You can take off. This is where you stay for now."

I struggle to remove the gag. My tongue is stuck to the roof of my mouth, but before he turns, I croak out, "How long?"

"Until we say."

Another man, older, almost elderly, shuffles down the stairs carrying a tray with bowls and bottles of water. "I am Hassan. You eat. You sleep. You stay quiet. If you scream, no more food or water or light. Understand?"

The three of us nod, and he sets the tray down on the floor.

And then...they all leave, the trap door shuts, and something heavy scrapes against the ceiling.

I run up the stairs as quietly as I can and push at the wood. It doesn't budge. We're trapped, and from what little of the house and the village I saw through my *boshiya*, no one will ever be able to find us here.

2

Joey

I JERK AWAKE, hitting my head on the wall behind me. It's stuffy. The mattresses are stained and smell like urine, so we're sleeping on the floor. Well, Mia and Ivy are sleeping on the floor. I'm pressed against the wall opposite the stairs, my knees drawn up to my chest, trying to make myself as small as possible. I can't let them sneak up on me. Or catch me unawares.

Jefe grabs my hair and yanks me off the floor, waking me from an exhausted sleep. I scream, but the other girls are powerless to help me. Emmie raises her head from where she lies across the railcar, in too much pain to move. She does what she can...holds my gaze while Jefe shoves my dirty, ripped skirt up over my ass. I try to send myself somewhere else. Somewhere safe and warm where no one hurts me. But like every other time...I fail.

I stifle a sob, fully back in the here and now, watching the stairs again. Across the room, Mia shoots me a sympathetic look. "Sleep a while, Joey," she whispers, trying not to wake Ivy. "I'll keep watch."

"Can't. Not now." I hug myself tightly, digging my fingers hard enough into my sides to leave bruises. I need to feel something other than abject terror and hopelessness. We're God knows where, the rest of our team murdered, and they've locked us away where no one will find us. I won't cry. Not in front of Ivy and Mia. They're so young. I remember how strong Emmie was—in the beginning—and how much I loved her for it. Now...she's dead. Her demons took her life, and inadvertently saved mine.

"How long have we been here?" Mia asks when Ivy sits up and rubs her eyes.

I shrug. "We've had two meals, but I'm so hungry, I don't think they're feeding us more than once a day." The bowls of stew with some sort of meat—goat I think—don't come with utensils, and we have to eat with our hands. The tiny sink only supplies brownish water, and we're all dirty, exhausted, and weak.

Ivy wrings her hands. "What are they going to do to us?"

I don't want to tell her. All I want to do is close my eyes and pretend I'm somewhere else. Like...back in San Diego before everything went to hell.

"When will you be back?" I ask Ford as we lie in bed together, naked, his hand stroking gently up and down my arm.

"Six months. I'll be able to call sometimes, but letters will always get to me." He presses a kiss to my temple, and I fight not to cry.

"I'll miss you. Promise me you won't do anything too stupid out there, Marine."

"Never, buttercup. I'm yours, and as soon as you graduate, we're going to make it official."

But we never got that chance. Never made love again. Only ever had one more night together before...my entire life turned into a nightmare. I focus on Mia and Ivy. Twenty-one and twenty-two. The age I was. Their eyes are swollen, their cheeks stained with tears.

"Listen..." I say softly, hoping my gentle tone will make the harsh words easier. "We're...women. In a country where many... consider us property. Whatever happens, be smart. Don't fight when there's no hope. Save your strength for any chance you have to get free. And if you see an opportunity, take it. Even if you have to go alone."

Heavy footsteps thud above us, and I snap my gaze to the top of the stairs. Ivy and Mia press deeper into the corner. After the scraping of whatever they use to cover the trapdoor, sunlight spills into the basement. Daytime. It doesn't last long, though. Two hulking forms lumber down the stairs. I don't know these men. They aren't the ones who took us. Bigger, meaner looking.

The lead one points at Ivy and Mia. "You two, up. You are coming with us."

I push to my feet, blinking hard to clear the dizziness threatening. As terrified as I am, I have to protect Ivy and Mia if I can, so they're going to take me first. But the man who appears to be in charge shakes his head. "Not you."

"Why not? Where are you taking them?"

"Away." The man shoves me back against the wall. "You make trouble, you get hurt."

Ivy and Mia haven't moved, and the other man strides over to them, grabs Mia's arm, and drags her towards the stairs as she screams and hits him with her free hand.

"Wait!" I beg. "Please. Give me a minute with them." I look up at the man looming over me, praying he'll relent. But he just knocks me to the side with a bulky arm and laughs as I fall to the floor. Mia's already up the stairs, and suddenly, her screams die down, and that's so much worse.

Ivy doesn't fight as she follows, just looks back at me. "Joey? What do we do?"

"Be strong," I say quietly as I rub my shoulder.

And when the trapdoor shuts and I'm alone, I realize what utter bullshit that advice is and start to cry.

Ford

From my corner office on the sixth floor, I look out over the Boston skyline. The morning sun is just about to peek over the horizon, and I lean back in my chair, waiting.

I used to love sunrise. My best memory—the one I pull up when everything else goes to shit—is of dawn on Pacific Beach, down on one knee with Joey practically glowing in the morning sun.

"I know it's only been a year, buttercup. And I'm leaving in a month. But...you're my sunshine. Marry me?"

The past few weeks, I can't stop thinking about her. Maybe it's knowing Wren found her forever. Her other half. Even if the guy is a brooding asshole.

Hell...what do I know? I've met him three times. But Ryker McCabe ghosted my best friend and boss, Dax, when he needed the guy most. I just don't know if I can forgive him for that.

Pulling up my email, I find a message from Wren. Good. My current client, the director of the Boston Museum of Art, suspects her husband is embezzling money from his brokerage firm, and while I've found plenty of shady behavior on the guy's part, I'm shit at the computer angle. That's all Wren.

Ford, here's everything I could find on Barry Martin. He's good—or has someone good covering his tracks—but no one has this many offshore accounts unless they're hiding something. Still digging. I have a line on a shell corporation I think I can trace to him. More this afternoon. How's things? Miss you. Seattle's great, though. It's actually a lot like Boston. All neighborhoods and traffic. You'd like it. Take care of Dax, will you? He's been...well... I can't tell him to call Ry. But maybe you can? -Wren

Dammit. When Ryker and Wren got back from Russia, Dax decided to forgive the guy for ghosting on him for six years after they both escaped Hell—a system of caves deep under a mountain in the Hindu Kush where the two of them were tortured. Fifteen months they spent there until Ryker escaped. The asshole in charge of Hell blinded Dax in revenge for the escape, and when Ryker came back to rescue him and found him unable to see, he couldn't deal with his guilt.

Dax's shocked swear booms down the hall, and I push away from my desk and take off at a run as Trevor starts frantically apologizing for something. *Now what?*

"Oh, shit." Sheer packing tape stretches from one side of the front office door to the other—except where it's stuck to Dax's face, hands, and arms. "Trev, what the hell were you thinking?" I ask as I start peeling the tape from Dax's glasses.

"That Clive needed payback for putting lube on my desk chair last week. I called Dax to warn him..."

"Thirty seconds before I walked into...what is this? Packing tape? It's not like I can see the damn stuff. No more pranks at the office. Period," Dax growls.

After a few minutes and lots of excuses, I manage to free my boss from the tape and press his cane back into his hand. He grunts something unintelligible, stalks off towards his office, and slams the door.

"You know you screwed up big time, right?" I ask Trevor.

His green eyes darken, and he drops his gaze to the floor, a huge wad of tape in his hands. "I called to warn him."

"Look, I know you and Clive always try to outdo one another. I get it. I used to pull that shit when I was enlisted. But you gotta think, man. Keep the pranks to ones Dax can avoid."

He offers me a wry smile. "So you're saying I should fight dirty?"

"No!" Trevor may be one of the scariest and deadliest men I've ever met—outside of Dax and Ryker—but he's only thirty-three. Practically a kid. And today, I've had about enough of his shit. "I'm saying keep it localized to Clive's office. No public areas. Ever again. Got it?"

His expression sobers, and he nods. "Understood. Sorry."

"I'm not the one you need to apologize to. But give him an hour or two. Otherwise you might not get out of his office alive." With a sigh, I head for the coffee pot as Trevor rushes back to his dark, windowless space next to the kitchen. As I pass Wren's old office, I frown. She was always the peacekeeper. Always the one who could make Dax stop and take a step back. Without her, it feels like we're all walking on eggshells.

Heading for Dax's office, I psych myself up for a fight.

Hours later, I walk our latest client to the door. Evianna Archer is a little skittish. Understandable, since she's being stalked, but all throughout that meeting, I felt like she was drawn to Dax, even though I'm the one handling her case.

Shake it off. She probably just responded to him because he's the owner. And he took the initial call. Whatever.

It's not like I'd start anything with her. Every relationship I've had—since Joey—has ended within weeks. No one else lives up to my memories of her.

"Marjorie," I say to our receptionist when we reach the front desk, "can you get Evianna set up with our billing system? Clive is going to follow her back to her office." With a quick check of my watch, I frown. The dude's taking his sweet time getting up here. "And book me from 6:00 a.m. to 8:00 a.m. and 6:00 p.m. to 9:00 p.m. every night for the rest of the week. Will that be appropriate for getting you to and from the office, Evianna?"

"Oh, yes." Her cheeks flush, like she doesn't want to be any trouble. "I can firm up my schedule this afternoon. I don't want you to have to wait in the lobby or outside my house for hours."

I soften my tone and lean an elbow on Marjorie's desk. "This is what we do, Evianna. A lot of PI work is waiting. And if you're not ready to leave, I can surveil or handle email on my phone until you're done."

"If you're sure..." She presses her lips together, the move highlighting the stress lines around her mouth. The woman's been through some shit in the past few days.

"I'm sure."

Clive ambles up, his leather jacket slung over his shoulders. After I introduce him and verify that Evianna has everything she needs, I make a beeline for the coffee machine. Dax is standing at the counter, a mug in his hands.

"Clive's following our new client back to her office," I say, pouring myself a cup of black gold. "Want some?"

Dax's brows draw inward, and he rubs the back of his neck as he extends his cup in my general direction. He may be blind, but he always seems to know exactly where I am. He and Ryker are absolutely creepy with echolocation.

"What do think about her...her case?" he asks.

Half of what Evianna talked about—home automation, code, data breaches—went completely over my head. "I wish we had Wren for this one," I admit.

Our phones vibrate simultaneously with a message from accounting. Evianna paid our retainer before she even got back to her office.

Removing his Bluetooth, Dax tucks the little earbud into his front pocket. "She pays on time. And I keep telling you. Wren's not dead. She's in Seattle. They have the internet there. Hell, she emailed me this morning asking when we'd have something new for her. Pull her in so we can wrap this up quickly."

"You don't like our new client." I follow him back to his

office where he sets his mug down on the center of the desk. There are days I'd swear the man wasn't blind. "Why not?"

"She clearly doesn't like me. That handshake was—"

I set down my mug before I double over with laughter as it hits me. Why the end of the meeting felt so off. Why she went from staring at Dax like he was a god to acting like he'd killed her puppy in the space of five minutes.

Dax arches a brow. "You didn't think she was a little... confrontational at the end?"

With a final snort, I get myself under control. After this morning, Dax isn't in the mood for my shit. "You're wearing your glasses."

"What's that have to do with anything? I needed the camera in the damn things to read me her police report. And I've had a low level headache for three days. They help with the light sensitivity."

"Look, I know you can't see yourself, but your glasses hide a lot of the scarring. And how pale your eyes really are. Evianna smiled at you a couple of times. You didn't respond. And when you held out your hand at the end? She was waiting for you to take hers. She doesn't know you're blind."

"And I came across as a total jerk?" He pulls off his glasses and pinches the bridge of his nose. "Shit."

His voice holds an odd note. Somewhere between longing and regret, and I study him for a minute. I think...he might be interested in her.

"I'll explain when I talk to her," I say as I head for the door. "Clive's going to handle everything until I can line up Ronan or Vasquez for the night shift. She didn't want close contact. Those two know how to be unobtrusive."

"Don't. Don't tell her anything about me. It's not important, and I don't want anyone's pity. She doesn't have to like me. She's a client. One I probably won't talk to again."

"Whatever you want." My phone buzzes with a number I

don't recognize, but the area code...is San Diego. "Shit," I say under my breath. "Gotta take this. Catch you tomorrow."

As soon as I'm out in the hall, I jab the screen. "Ford Lawton. Who's calling?"

"Ford?" The voice is vaguely familiar, but I can't place the soft, scratchy tone. "This is Geraldine. Gerry Taylor. Joey's older sister."

My heart stops, but my legs are still moving, carrying me back to my office where I shut the door. "Gerry? How did you even get this number? What's wrong?"

"I...I asked a friend of mine—a local cop, retired now—to track you down. Joey's missing."

I don't hear anything for another minute, and then my back is pressed to the door and my ass is resting on the hardwood. "Missing?" The word scrapes over my throat, like if I don't say it, maybe it won't be true. "From where? For how long? Tell me everything."

THE OFFICE WALLS press in on me as I scour our various intel sources on Turkmenistan.

Human trafficking.

Two hundred women reported missing in the last two years.

Turkmenistan authorities increase border security to stop trafficking of women into Iraq and Afghanistan.

Closing my eyes, I see Joey. Scared. Abused. Bloodied. Twenty-two, and kidnapped to be sold down in Mexico. Because I wouldn't talk to her.

If she's in trouble now—if she *has* been taken by traffickers —I have to do something. I have to find her.

Pushing to my feet, I grab my jacket from the back of the door. I have to make some calls, and I do *not* want these records on Second Sight's phone bill.

SINKING DOWN into my recliner with a brand new burner phone from the local Stop-N-Shop, I dial numbers I memorized twelve years ago when I left the Marines. I don't even know if Nomar's still alive, let alone using this number. But I have to try.

"Identify yourself," the rough voice with the hint of a Spanish accent says.

"Master Sergeant Ford Lawton. U.S. Marine Corps. Retired."

"Where'd we meet, Marine?"

I close my eyes, resting my head against the back of the chair. "Al-Faw Peninsula. Satisfied now, Lone Ranger?"

Nomar chuckles. "How the fuck are you, Ford?"

"Not good." The coffee burns my throat, but I doubt I'll be sleeping any time soon, and it's either this or suck down gin and tonics until I'm dead to the world. "I need some intel. You still running covert ops in—"

"This better be a fucking secure line if you want to finish that sentence..."

"It's a burner phone run through multiple anonymizers. How much more secure you want me to be, asswipe?" Slamming the coffee cup down on the end table, I watch, unable to move, as some of the black liquid splashes over the rim and drips onto my beige carpet.

"Take a pill, man. Yes. I'm still in charge of ops in Uzbek-istan." Nomar sighs over the line, and for a minute, I feel ancient.

I remember when calling overseas meant the perpetual hiss of static and long delays after every sentence. "Five days ago, a Doctors Without Borders group went dark outside of Sayat. They were headed for Turkmenabat, but they never got there."

"Shit. And they hired *you*?" Nomar's whistle grates along my spine.

"No." Clearing my throat, I lean forward and lower my voice. As if whispering will somehow make what I have to say untrue. "I know—knew—one of the doctors. We...fuck. We were engaged back in our twenties. She's missing, Nomar, along with six others. I have to find her. And I need your help to do it."

3

Ford

WITH EVERY PASSING MINUTE, the tension gathering between my shoulder blades intensifies, and by the time I stand in front of Dax's door, it feels like there's a knife digging into my back.

Dax looks like hell, and the apartment is completely dark when I stride through the door. "VoiceAssist: Lights on, sixty percent. It's after eight, Dax."

He shrugs and ambles into the kitchen, his limp a little more pronounced than I've seen it lately.

"Beer?" he asks.

"Sure." I can't force out more than a one word answer, and he arches a brow, highlighting the scars around his eyes.

"What's wrong?"

I take the bottle and follow him to his spartan living room before sinking into a single chair across from him. "You're scary, you know that?" After a swig of beer, I let out a long, slow breath. "I thought I was hiding it pretty well."

"It's in your voice. Spill." He drapes his arm across the back of the couch and stares straight through me. Despite not being able to see, he always knows right where to look. It's like he's seeing into my soul.

"Joey's missing."

"Joey?" Leaning forward, he shakes his head. "Sorry, but who is he?"

Anger stiffens my spine, and I push to my feet and start pacing the room, needing to do something...*anything*...to distract me from the images running through my mind—all the things those assholes could be doing to her right now. "She." I pause for another sip of beer before I clarify. "Josephine Taylor? The woman I was dating when I joined the marines?"

"Don't you mean the woman who dumped you when you joined the marines?" Dax says, his voice taking on a harsh tone.

Shit. Maybe I have a little more...baggage surrounding Joey than I thought if that's what he remembers from our conversations about her. "Well, sort of. I mean...no." Swallowing hard over the lump in my throat, I start to pace again. "Her sister called me. No one's heard from Joey in ten days. She was working for Doctors Without Borders in Turkmenistan, and the whole group's just...gone."

"Shit. Turkmenistan's a war zone, Ford. If she got caught between a couple of the local factions, she's not missing. She's in a shallow grave somewhere."

"Don't you think I know that?" I snap.

Dax flinches and throws his hands up in surrender as I clutch the bottle so hard, I worry it's going to crack. "Sorry. Is the CIA involved? Any demands for ransom?"

Anger turns to pure, unadulterated rage as I recount my call with one of Trevor's contacts two hours ago. "The CIA won't investigate. Something about not wanting to upset the fragile peace in the region. Total bullshit. And Doctors Without Borders doesn't even know where the group was before they went missing. They were in some remote region where their SAT phone didn't work properly. Their last known location was somewhere outside of Sayat, but they were heading to Turkmenabat."

Sinking back down into the leather chair, I lean forward, my elbows on my knees. "I can't just leave her out there, Dax. I owe her that much."

"You don't owe her anything. She couldn't handle dating a marine on active duty and she bailed."

The sound escaping my throat is more like a growl than a sigh, and I roll my eyes. "No. She didn't. She stayed with me for almost a year. I proposed before I left for my first oversees assignment. We wrote letters, even talked on the phone a couple of times. But...then I got three days leave. Back home in San Diego. And I didn't call her."

Dax arches his brow. "So, let me guess. You were out with the guys, drinking until you were shit-faced, wearing your whites to impress the ladies, and she just happens to walk into the bar with her girlfriends to find you with a pretty little thing on your lap."

Bristling because he's both right and wrong, I roll my head to try to relieve some of the tension. "I wasn't shit-faced. That came later," I say quietly. "Never touched another woman. Never even looked. All my mates were trying to hook up with anything that moved. Me? I just sat at the bar. Nursing a drink. For three fucking hours."

"Why?" Something flashes over Dax's face. Longing. Pain. Frustration. But he takes a sip of his beer and waits for me to continue.

Staring up at the ceiling, I send myself back twenty years to that damn bar the night I lost everything. "It was war, Dax. We were dropped in country after only six weeks of basic. The day before we got the news they were rotating us home...I killed six hostiles. One of them used a couple of kids as a human shield. The day before, we were a few blocks away when a suicide bomber took out a public market. Kids. Babies. Innocents. Joey didn't deserve thirty-six hours of me crying and asking her why."

"And did you tell her that?"

"Nope. I fucked up. And it cost her...more than I can explain. Because of me, she was in the wrong place at the wrong time, and...shit. It was bad, Dax." I can't tell him what happened to her. It's not my place. "She tried to reach out... after...but I was on mission for almost six weeks, and I didn't get her message until it was over. By then...it was too late. I wrote her letters trying to explain, apologizing, begging her to talk to me, but she returned every damn one of them. Unopened. Eventually...I stopped."

After Dax takes a long sip of beer, he asks, "What are you going to do?"

"I have a contact in Uzbekistan—Nomar—who's trying to slip unnoticed into Turkmenistan. If so—or if he can get in touch with some of his contacts there—he'll check out their last known location, retrace the route they were supposed to follow. He'll contact me tomorrow."

"And then?"

As if he has to ask. "If there's a chance she's alive...I'm going to find her." Setting my bottle down on the coffee table harder than I intend, I blow out a breath. "But that means I need you to find someone else to take over the Archer case. Or...at least run point on it with me until I hear back from Nomar."

Dax squeezes his eyes shut and presses the cold bottle of beer to his temple. "There isn't anyone else. Ella's tied up on that embezzlement case. Trevor can handle the basic surveillance on days, and Vasquez at night with Ronan as backup, but Clive messaged me right before I left the office. His mom's about to have open-heart surgery."

"Fuck."

With a sigh, he shakes his head. "First thing in the morning, read me in with what you have so far. If you need to leave, take Trevor, and I'll run point with Wren until Clive returns."

We finish our beers in silence, and when he walks me to the door, I clear my throat. If I'm going to go dark on him—and abandon a client—I have to come clean. "I never stopped loving her, Dax."

"Then you'll get her back." He grabs my forearm, squeezes once, and gives me a final nod. "But until we know more, don't tell Evianna I'm involved with her case. No need to worry her until we know there's something to worry about."

What the hell is he so concerned about? I'm about to ask when a sudden flash of memory—Joey in my bed, looking up at me with such love in her eyes—distracts me. "Whatever you say. I'll see you in the morning." Halfway down the hall, I turn. "Thank you."

Joey

For what feels like an hour, I've been shaking, rocking back and forth as loud footsteps thunder over my head. Angry voices shout, and something heavy crashes to the ground.

Hamid has brought me two meals since they took Ivy and Mia. Two days. All alone in this dingy, stuffy basement. And yet, I don't know if I should wish I were with them. My heart breaks for what they might be going through. They're young. Pretty. Just the type to be sold for a premium price. Me...? At forty-two, maybe I don't rate so high. But then...why did they take me? Why not just kill me?

Pulling the paperclip from my pocket, I scrap it across my inner arm, hard enough to draw blood.

I tried to resist. Tried to keep the pressure light. But it's either cut myself again or let the fear drown me. I've been treading water for days, and I'm so tired.

As crimson wells on my skin, then starts to roll towards my wrist, I let out a quiet whimper. A single tear escapes down my cheek. The first time I cut myself, I was twenty-two and still in the hospital after the police rescued me. The last? Two years ago. When the power went out at my apartment and I woke up in pitch blackness.

No one's touched me. Not once. No one's even talked to me. I tried to ask Hamid about Ivy and Mia, but he just shook his head and grunted for me to keep quiet.

The loud noises cease, and a second cut...this one to my inner thigh, lets me breathe again. After the last meal, I took a chance and used the lukewarm, brown water from the sink to wash my underwear and pants. The idea of giving up my underwear for even an hour left me shaking and nauseous, but I couldn't stand my own stench anymore. Every time I inhaled, I was right back inside that railcar.

At least I still have the *abaya* covering me.

The silence doesn't last long. Footsteps head for the trap door, then the scraping sound of whatever hides it follows. I spring up, my joints aching from disuse, lack of sleep, and so little food, and I sprint for the sink where I draped my clothes.

They're still damp, but I'll be damned if I let these men anywhere near me wearing only the abaya. The fabric clings to my skin as I struggle back into the pants and I barely manage to zip them up before the door bangs open.

Hamid thunders down the steps, an angry string of words in a language I don't understand flying from his lips. Full-Beard chases him, and when Hamid reaches me, cowering against the wall, he backhands me, hard, then whirls on Full-Beard and berates him as I cup my throbbing cheek.

"You are trouble," Hamid spits at me, then yanks up my *abaya* and paws at my pants as I kick and scratch and try to fight him off. "You brought them here. You and the other two whores."

"Our orders say she is not to be touched," Full-Beard growls, and then Hamid's weight disappears, and he hits the wall a few feet away. "We will be gone within the hour. Go upstairs. Now."

Hamid continues to mutter in his native language as he limps back up to the main floor, and Full-Beard looks down at me. "Hands."

"What's going on?" I ask.

"Hands!" He reaches down and grabs my wrist, jerking me to my feet and then shoving me against the wall. I can't offer him my hands fast enough, and he duct tapes my wrists again, gags me, and pulls the *boshiya* over my head.

"Sit. Wait."

I don't have a choice, so I sink back down to the ground, the *boshiya* shrouding the room in semi-darkness, and try not to hyperventilate. Not more than ten minutes later, No-Beard and Full-Beard stomp down the stairs, followed by two other men I don't recognize. Their coloring is a little different. Darker, smoother skin. Slicker hair. Better clothing.

One of the new men takes my arm and pulls me up. He's not gentle, but not exactly rough either, and he leads me up the stairs behind Full-Beard, through the house, where Hamid makes a rude gesture, and out to a different, slightly smaller van.

Full-Beard opens the back doors and pulls up a false floor in the van to reveal a compartment—maybe two feet deep, six feet long, and three feet wide. "Put her in there," he says to the man holding me.

No. Anywhere but in there.

I plead through the gag, sobbing, but it does no good. The one holding me scoops me up and lays me in the compartment. "You will be silent, or we will make you be silent. This is the only way over the border. Do you understand? He wants you alive and able to work, but he said nothing about causing you pain."

My vision starts to tunnel, but I nod. What choice do I have? There are four of them, one of me, and I'm bound, weak, and terrified. As the lid of the storage compartment slides closed, I give in to the darkness pulling me under, and everything around me fades away.

A SLIGHT BREEZE through the black mesh of the *boshiya* dries the tears and sweat staining my cheeks, and I force myself to come back from wherever my battered mind sent me when they locked me in this compartment. I only know it was dark and hot and full of so much pain.

One of my newer captors, a man with a skinny face and a groomed beard holds out his hand. "Out. We are over the border." His English is excellent, better than any of the others, and I raise my bound wrists, wincing as my shoulders, back, and legs all protest the forced confinement.

He's almost careful as he maneuvers me against the wall of the van, then slides the metal flooring back into place. The rear door is open, and I try to see around him to orient myself. The movement sends pain singing up my arm, and a choked sob escapes—all I can manage through the gag.

"Keep her quiet," Full-Beard snaps.

The man kneeling next to me shakes his head and mutters something under his breath in Pashto before switching to English. "Are you thirsty?" He's so much more...refined than Full-Beard and No-Beard. Like he's...above them somehow.

I nod, then wish I hadn't as the interior of the van starts to spin. I'm so dizzy, I don't even notice when he lifts the *boshiya* and loosens the gag. But then a bottle of water is pressed to my lips, and I grab it, sucking down as much as I can.

"I'm...Joey. Who are you?" I can't keep making up names for these guys, and if I have any hope of getting out of this mess, I need to try to make my kidnappers see me as a person.

"Zaman."

Zaman. He seems...nicer than the others, so I risk another question. "Where are you taking me?"

"To the Amir Faruk," he says, as if that's supposed to explain everything.

My hands start to shake, and I can't stop myself from asking him every single question running through my mind. "Who is the Amir Faruk? And why did he have us kidnapped? I'm an American. He can't do this. Where are my friends? Someone took them away days ago—"

Zaman snatches the empty water bottle from my hands, yanks me to my feet, and drags me out of the van. "You will learn to be respectful. You belong to the Amir now."

Cutting the tape from my wrists, he shoves me off to the side of the road. "You piss now or you will sit in it. We have another eight hours before you get to your new home."

Eight hours. My new home?

As I relieve myself with Zaman watching my every move, I pray whoever was looking for us at Hamid's house knows where I am. Or where Ivy and Mia are. But when Zaman grabs my wrists and binds them together again, gags me, and pushes the *boshiya* over my head, I clench my hands hard enough my short nails dig into my palms. A tiny trickle of blood wells under one of my fingers, and I let the pain overtake all of my thoughts. The van speeds off as I huddle on the floor, Zaman and two other men with guns watching me like I'm a lamb headed for the slaughter.

4

Ford

THERE ISN'T enough coffee in the world this morning. Still, the scent wafting from my large to-go cup helps with the exhaustion. Lying awake all night didn't leave me in the best shape to guard our newest client on her way to work. Nor did the 5:00 a.m. phone call from Nomar.

Four dead. Buried in shallow graves. All men.

A sick feeling claws up my from my stomach, lingering in the back of my throat. So of course, I do the dumbest thing possible—take a swig of coffee.

Less than a minute later, I'm bent over a garbage can, heaving up what little I've managed to drink in the past half an hour. If Joey's still alive...

Get your shit together. You're no good to her if you can't even keep coffee down. Plus, you have a client to take care of first.

Pulling a bottle of water from my bag, I rinse my mouth out, toss the remains of the coffee in the trash, and pop a couple of mints. Only another few hours and I can focus on Joey. Find her. Until then, I have to take care of business.

Evianna locks her front door and takes off at a good clip towards the T station. I told her where I was, but she still keeps checking behind her—probably trying to catch sight of me. At a stoplight, I text her.

Ford: *Stop looking for me. Act normal.*

As I follow her through the turnstile and wait on the platform, she responds.

Evianna: *Being stalked isn't exactly "normal" for me. Neither is having a bodyguard. You try acting normal with a giant, lethal-looking dude following you.*

Despite the stress turning my shoulders into solid blocks of granite, I chuckle.

Ford: *Think of me as a really tall teddy bear. Who knows how to fight. Dax and Trevor are the lethal ones.*

The train is full, and I can barely see Evianna at the other end of the car, but anyone after her would be an idiot to try something in front of all of these people, so I relax a bit and let the rhythmic sound and vibrations relax me. I know this town. Know my job.

The trip to Evianna's office is uneventful, and I lengthen my stride to catch her right before the elevator doors close, then punch the buttons for every floor between the lobby and her office. It's the best I can do under the circumstances to give myself time to talk to her without showing my face to her coworkers.

"Sorry, I needed a minute."

Her eyes widen, a hint of fear creeping into her tone. "Is something wrong?"

Yes. Something is very wrong.

"Not exactly. It's nothing to do with your case. But I have an emergency I have to take care of. You're not leaving the office today?"

"No. It's crunch time. We're getting sandwiches delivered

and it's all hands on deck. I won't leave until eight." With a little huff, she adjusts her briefcase. "Hell, if I didn't have to worry about scheduling with you, I might stay until midnight. But I can pack up at eight and finish up the night at home."

Running a hand through my hair, I hope this won't destroy all of her confidence in Second Sight. But I don't have a choice. "Okay. The Dunkin' Donuts right next door is open until ten. I have to coordinate with the rest of the team, but I'll send someone there at eight to meet you. I'll text you their photo once I figure out who's free."

The doors slide shut on the fourth floor, and the next stop is Beacon Hill. "Ford?" When I meet her gaze, she squeezes my arm. "I hope everything's okay."

"Me too, Evianna. Thanks for understanding."

It only takes me ten minutes to walk to Second Sight from Evianna's building, and I spend the entire time on the phone with Nomar. He's working half a dozen angles right now, trying to figure out where they might have taken Joey and the other two women, but he's hitting walls left and right.

"I found their convoy. There's evidence of sabotage. Three out of the four tires on the lead vehicle had been patched, and the fourth was slashed. I don't think they had time to repair it before they were ambushed. It looks like they stopped for the night, set up camp, and were taken from there. It's been at least five days, though. No footprints, vehicle tracks...nothing left. Too much wind destroying the evidence. My only reference is body decomp." Nomar stifles a yawn. "Sorry, man. I haven't slept since you called me."

"What do you need? What do *we* need?" I yank open the building's outer door and head for the stairs. Maybe the exercise will help break up some of this tension banding its way around my forehead.

"Don't you have someone working for you who used to be a spook?" Nomar asks.

"Yeah. Trevor Moana. He was a Targeting Officer for ten years."

A muffled curse carries over the line, and then Nomar clears his throat. "We need him. If he has any contacts in this area, it'll help. And I need money. The only way to get shit done over here is to grease the right palms."

"How much?" Nodding to Marjorie, I head for my office to drop off my briefcase.

"Ten grand."

"Just tell me where you want it and consider it done. Once I talk to Dax and Trevor, I'll let you know our ETA."

"Get here safe, Marine," Nomar says before the call clicks and goes silent.

Having a plan eases some of my nausea. "I'm coming for you, buttercup," I say quietly before I head for Dax's office to fill him in.

The small lines of tension around his eyes deepen as I tell him all three women are missing and the four men were shot.

"The locals told Nomar stories of their daughters going missing." After a pause, I swallow over the lump in my throat. "Nomar's waiting for me at the Uzbeki border." I don't know how to ask for what I need, and I tighten my grip on the arms of the chair until my knuckles crack.

"Take Trevor with you," Dax says, and my body feels like a balloon someone just let all the air out of. "And...I'll call Ryker. Doesn't matter who has Joey, he and his team...they can get her out."

"Dax—" I don't know what to say. Bringing in Ryker isn't something I want to be responsible for. Dax would have to coordinate, and he'd be forced to confront his demons. As much as I think he needs to, that has to happen on his own terms. Otherwise, it's asking for trouble.

"I talked to Ry last night. Couple of hours after you left. This is what he does, Ford. K&R. Let me help. I can't...go with you. But I can do this."

The pain in his voice echoes what's in my heart. I'll never understand exactly how hard it is for him to stay behind a desk. He's former Special Forces—used to being the one making things happen. And now, he can't do more than coordinate from here. Even that requires adaptive, specialized equipment.

I lean forward. "Let me get there first. Get the lay of the land. I'll take Trevor. He's got contacts all over the Middle East. But..." I pull the chair closer, "we were already understaffed this week. And if I take Trevor, there's no one to watch Evianna. Unless you want to pull Ronan or Vasquez off nights."

Dax shakes his head. "Ronan's too green. He's only been with us for a month. He's fine as a backup to Vasquez, but not on his own. Not with a guy who's escalating to violence." Rubbing his neck, he huffs. "You do realize asking a blind man to step in as bodyguard is fucking ridiculous, right?"

A hint of the man he was before Ryker came back and set him on edge returns, and I choke out a laugh. "Maybe."

My phone buzzes. "Shit," I say quietly. "Nomar arranged for transpo from Turkey. But I have to be there in thirty-six hours. I typed up the case notes first thing this morning. They're in your inbox."

Dax pushes to his feet and steps around his desk. When I stand, he offers me his hand, then pulls me close enough he has to crane his neck look up at me. For some reason, he wants me to see his eyes, even if he can't see mine. "Promise me one thing."

"What?"

"Don't go dark on me. Check in, and if you need help, you let me call Ry."

I can't tell him how much his support means to me. Not now, when all I can think about is Joey. So I pull him in for a quick hug. He stiffens, but doesn't resist.

"Be safe," he says as I head for the door. "And get her back alive."

"I'm going to try."

If I don't, I won't be able to live with myself.

Joey

By the time the van rolls to a stop, I can't feel my fingers, my butt is numb from sitting in one position for hours, and the tight gag has rubbed the corners of my mouth raw.

Zaman glared at me for most of the trip. Whoever he is, he's very protective of this Amir Faruk. He was almost kind when offering me the water—even when he put me in that horrible hidden compartment. But as soon as I started asking questions, his entire demeanor changed.

The back doors of the van open, and Zaman yanks me to my feet. My legs won't hold me, and I start to fall, but he catches me and slings me over his shoulder.

I try to tell him to put me down—the sensation of his arm pressing against the backs of my thighs makes me want to vomit, but he grunts at me to be quiet and strides through a set of thick, wooden double doors.

Too caught up in my memories and fears to notice the exterior of the building, I'm almost shocked when bright, electric lights illuminate a lavish foyer. The scent of spices perfumes the air, and what little I can see of the floor speaks of wealth.

Smooth, polished red tiles, and a thick area rug under Zaman's feet pass by.

Terrified I'm about to find out why this Amir Faruk wants me, I shake in Zaman's grip, fighting not to cry. I miss Ivy and Mia. Even though we weren't close, they were so innocent, so...*happy*. They have their whole lives ahead of them. Or did... I don't even know if they're still alive.

Me...if my kidnappers kill me, maybe...it'll be easier. Easier than having another violent man lock me up, use me for his pleasure, or torture me.

Zaman sets me down, and I stumble backwards, crashing into a massive wall of muscle. By the curse, it's Full-Beard. He doesn't help me right myself, and I almost land on my ass, but manage to find my balance at the last minute.

A deep voice, heavily accented but in perfect English, snaps, "This is the doctor?"

The *boshiya* is ripped off my head, and I blink in the suddenly bright lights. My blond hair is a mess, matted and dirty, and as rough hands untie the gag, a few strands are torn from my scalp.

My eyes adjust, and then I can't tear my gaze away from the man in front of me. He's tall—maybe six-foot-two—thin, with a perfectly trimmed beard and pale gray eyes. His loose blue pants and tunic look expensive and pressed, despite the late hour.

"Dr. Josephine Taylor. My name is Amir Abdul Faruk. You will address me as Amir Faruk or Sir."

Sir? Who the hell does this guy think he is?

The second that thought crosses my mind, I lower my eyes. If he sees the hatred and fear written across my face, I don't know what he'll do. Not that I think my little act of submission is going to save me.

"Did you hear me, *spei*?" Faruk says sharply. "I will not be disrespected in my home by a *woman*."

He slaps me across the face, and I crash to my knees, my bound hands hitting the floor so hard, I feel the impact all the way up my arms. "Yes, Amir Faruk," I whisper as I struggle to my feet.

"That is better." His voice softens, and I risk a quick peek up at him. "I do not wish to harm you."

His lies grate, and my anger boils over, tamping down my fear and loosening my tongue. "You just hit me, you bastard. You kidnapped us, killed the rest of our group, and took my friends away! No one will tell me where they are or what happened to them—" This time when his hand flies, I manage to stay on my feet, but I taste blood. "Whatever you're going to do to me...just get it over with. *Sir.*"

Faruk chuckles as he circles me. "You are a brave woman, Josephine. Perhaps not as smart as I expected. But no matter." When he's standing in front of me again, he calls, "Isaad!"

I try not to flinch at his shout, and a moment later, a tall, pale man hurries in. His shoulders slump, and if I had to bet, I'd say he's not from Afghanistan. His blue eyes are rounder, and his entire demeanor says he's uncomfortable in his own skin.

"Yes, sir?" Isaad says quietly. His accent is hard to identify, but it's definitely not the same as Faruk's or Zaman's. Conflict churns in his gaze as he looks from Faruk to me and back again.

"Erase all evidence of Dr. Josephine Taylor from public records in America. She does not exist anymore." Faruk passes Isaad my passport, and I lunge for it, so desperate, I don't think about the consequences.

Pain explodes down my legs and across my scalp as Zaman grabs my hair and kicks me in the back of the knees to send me to the floor. "Please," I beg, holding up my bound hands. "You can't just make me disappear!"

"I can. Very easily," Faruk says with a smile that makes my skin crawl. "Your *friends* will be sold in two days. They are being prepared for auction as we speak. You, however, are too valuable to let go."

Sold. Trafficked. Used. I want to throw up. Isaad stares at me, pain welling in the depths of his eyes, then lowers his gaze to the floor, turns, and rushes from the room.

I suck in a breath through my teeth, trying to chase the dizziness away. My stomach flips and twists as I wobble to my feet. "Wh-why...? They were helping save lives. They're good kids. But they're just...*kids*. Twenty-three and twenty-four. Please, don't—"

"Lisette!" Faruk calls, all patience now gone from his tone. "Bring my son."

A woman—beautiful, but with fear in her dark green eyes—hurries into the room with a child trailing behind her. He looks to be around six or seven, and his skin is pale—almost yellow—his wispy hair sticking to his sweaty forehead and his free arm wrapped around his stomach.

"This is my son. Mateen has what is known as Alpha Thalassemia. You will attend to him. He needs regular blood transfusions, among other treatments, until you are able to cure him."

Shock slackens my jaw. He kidnapped me to help a child? "H-he needs to be in a hospital."

Faruk spits at my feet. "No. *You* will care for him. Here. He is my only son and the doctors in Kandahar do not specialize in this disease. You do."

"Clearly—*sir*—you've done your research on Alpha Thalassemia. So you know how serious it can be." I focus on Mateen. He moans quietly, his face pressed to his mother's arm, but his bloodshot and red-rimmed eyes peeking up at me. Alpha Thalassemia can be fatal, and by the looks of the boy, he hasn't been receiving proper treatment. I straighten my spine and force strength into my voice. "Blood transfusions will only keep the disease from getting worse. He needs a bone marrow transplant."

Snapping his fingers at Zaman, Faruk says something I don't understand. After he digs in his satchel for a moment, Zaman passes me a thin sheaf of papers.

"I have your research, *doctor*. You wrote about a drug cocktail that can cure this disease without a transplant. I have secured an ample supply of everything you will need, and enough O negative blood to keep Mateen from worsening while you concoct the cure."

"I wrote this seven years ago," I protest. "It's all theory. No one's ever tested this. It's too risky. There's a reason this never went beyond the paper stage. A bone marrow transplant is safe. This...if anything goes wrong—even if everything goes right—the treatment could kill Mateen!"

"No," Faruk shouts. "There will be no transplant. You will treat him, and you will cure him. Or you will die." With a nod to Zaman, he barks out an order to Lisette, who flees from the room with Mateen.

I'm grabbed from behind, spun around, and pushed towards the door we entered through.

Struggling to free myself from Zaman's painful grip does me no good. He steers me down a set of stairs, through several turns and a long hallway, and into a small suite with a bed, a nightstand, a single lamp, and a tiny bathroom.

Several sets of folded clothes sit on top of the woven blankets on the bed, and an alarm clock, four bottles of water, and three granola bars rest on the nightstand. My stomach twists in on itself. I'm so hungry, the sight of food makes me dizzy.

Zaman pushes me down onto the bed, takes my hands, and cuts the duct tape from my wrists. Before I can rise, Faruk enters the room, blocking the doorway. "Tomorrow morning at 9:00 a.m., Zaman will come to collect you. If you are not ready to start work on the cure, you will suffer the consequences."

I'm too shocked to say a word as he and Zaman leave, but when the door slams, I race for it, slapping the wood with my palms as a heavy lock *thunks*. There's no handle, and I sink to the ground, tears burning my eyes. Ivy and Mia...they're going to be *sold*. And me? My research was all theoretical. There's no way a drug cocktail can cure Mateen. He'll die, and Faruk will kill me.

5

Joey

I DON'T KNOW how long I stay curled on the floor, but eventually, I push myself to my knees. Despite my exhaustion and hunger, I force myself to scour the room for any sort of weapon.

Nothing. Well, except for the toothbrush, but after days trapped with nothing but a sputtering sink offering brackish water, I'm so desperate to have clean teeth again, I abandon my search and spend ten minutes brushing until my gums bleed.

Catching sight of myself in the mirror, I quickly avert my eyes. I've lost at least ten pounds. My hair looks like the world's worst wig, and my eyes are sunken and bruised from all the crying.

The desire for a shower is almost overwhelming, but I'm so tired. So hungry. So scared. A quick check of the clock tells me it's close to midnight, and apparently I have to be ready at 9:00 a.m. in the morning, so I sink down onto the mattress and rip into the first granola bar. It's stale, but it tastes better than anything I've ever eaten.

It takes all the willpower I have not to eat through the

whole stash. With how little they've fed me, if I have more than one, I'll probably be sick. And who knows how long I need to make three remaining bars last. So instead, I wash the dry crumbs down with half a bottle of water, then take the pillow and move to the door.

I want to lie down in that bed. To sleep like a normal person. But...I can't. I can't let anyone sneak up on me. In the dark place...the place before the police came, the traffickers' favorite trick was to wait until one of us was sleeping, then grab us by the hair and force themselves on us. I won't let that happen again. If Faruk or his men try to use me, I'll fight with everything I have—even if it kills me. And I'm damn sure going to see it coming.

With my back to the door, I set the alarm for seven and close my eyes. The pillow feels so nice, and it's been so long since I've slept, but every half an hour or so, I jerk awake, convinced someone's coming for me. Footsteps outside, the odd creak of the walls or the slamming of a door somewhere above me...each sound could be the last I hear.

At least I'm not in the dark. The lamp by the bed casts a yellowish glow and the bathroom tiles almost shine in the light of the harsh, naked bulb hanging over the sink. The barest hint of comfort in this terrifying new reality.

Staring at the clock only makes me feel worse, so I turn it face down and give up trying to be strong. Hot tears stain my cheeks, and I pray for just an hour of sleep where my nightmares won't find me.

―――――――――

THE ALARM JOLTS me out of a nightmare—a large blob coming towards me, shapeless, faceless, absorbing me until there's nothing left. No emotion. No fight. No will to live.

I have two hours before they come—if Faruk was telling the

truth. On edge, but more awake than I've been in several days, I re-examine the room, looking for cameras. Nothing obvious, but the ceiling is made of wooden planks, and there are small gaps between a few of them.

In the bathroom, I find two rough towels and use one to cover the mirror. I'm filthy, and so desperate to be clean again. The water is only lukewarm, but it's mostly clear, and with one last look around the tiny room, I screw up my courage and discard my stained and ripped clothing before stepping under the flow.

The shampoo smells like flowers—not totally unpleasant—and I lather my hair three times before I feel like I've finally removed the dirt, sweat, and blood from the past...however long it's been.

The new scratches on my arm and inner thigh are mostly healed, but one of them still stings, and the pain helps me focus.

Survive. Fight. Find a way out.

I brush my teeth again and wrap myself in the second towel before checking out the clothes. Three sets: a burnt orange, a dark brown, and a garish yellow. I swallow my tears as I put on the plain, serviceable white bra and panties. I want to go home. But I'm terrified I'll never see the United States again. Choosing the orange, the least awful color, I pull on the pants. They're loose from my unintentional weight loss, but otherwise fit almost perfectly. As does the long-sleeved tunic. Even the soft slippers are the right size. Of course they are. He planned this. Planned to grab me.

My hospital published a news story about my trip—noteworthy because Turkmenistan hasn't allowed an aid mission in more than ten years. Faruk knew I'd be there, knew I'd be vulnerable.

Somehow, when I thought this was all a case of wrong place/wrong time, it was easier to handle. I didn't realize until just now how tightly I was clinging to the idea that maybe I'd be ransomed. That perhaps the government would intervene. But Faruk planned everything. And from the little I saw of the compound last night, it's huge—and well-guarded.

The clothes feel so much nicer than I want against my skin. I should hate everything about this place. But after a week in the same cotton t-shirt and rough black pants, the *abaya* and *boshiya* smothering me, this is like heaven.

Several dull-tipped hairpins rest on top of the black hijab, and I arrange the material to hide my damp locks and secure it in place.

My paperclip! I can't lose it, and I don't trust Faruk not to take my old clothes. They should probably be burned anyway given how dirty they are. Tucking the paperclip into my bra, I tear into one of the granola bars and down another bottle of water just as the clock ticks over to nine.

My heart leaps into my throat at the heavy footsteps in the hall, and when the lock *thunks* open, I press myself against the bed. Zaman looms in the doorway. "Follow me," he says, his dark eyes cold.

"Where are you taking me?"

Lunging forward, he grabs my arm in a vise grip, dragging me down the hall. "Where I say. If you make trouble, all of those nice things in your room will disappear very quickly."

Nice things?

Panic steals my focus until we reach the stairs and he releases my arm. The muscle throbs, and I try to rub the ache away as I trail meekly behind him. Down another corridor, he turns to the left and enters a large, sunny room filled with half a dozen women, including Lisette.

The high windows and glimpse of clear, blue sky send longing flooding through my limbs. Besides the few minutes spent outside the van to pee, I haven't seen the sun since we were taken.

Zaman points to a cushion positioned at the far corner of a large, rectangular tablecloth spread out on the floor. "Sit."

His harsh voice leaves me little hope he'll tolerate any questions without hurting me, so I press my lips together before I get myself in more trouble. Mirroring the other women's positions, I sink down onto the thin pillow and cross my legs. A tiny slip of a girl dressed all in black scurries into the room and offers me a plate with several thin rounds of bread on it, then gestures to several bowls on the tablecloth filled with what looks like thick pudding.

"Dip," she says quietly before rushing off.

"That is Asal," Lisette says. "She cooks for us. Eat. He will come soon."

The other women talk in hushed tones, sneaking glances at me, and I at them. Using one of the rounds of bread as a scoop, I try the pudding, which is vaguely lemony. Some sort of curd, perhaps.

What I see in the gazes all around me twists my stomach into a knot.

They're broken. Afraid. One has a black eye, another's cheek is swollen and purple in a mirror to my own. Dressed richly, most with jewels on their fingers and stacks of gold bangles on their wrists, they take small portions from a handful of different dishes. Eggs, rice, fruits... It's surreal. We're surrounded by luxury, but I think these women are just as trapped as I am.

I can only manage a few bites before I start to feel nauseous and push the plate away. What the hell am I supposed to do now?

Lisette tenses with a sharp intake of breath, my only warning before Zaman appears at my side and wraps his rough fingers around my arm. I yelp as he hauls me up, his tight grip bruising my already swollen flesh.

"Pay attention," he grunts as he marches me out of the

room, down another hallway, and through the lavish foyer to a set of ornate double doors. Releasing my arm, he throws the doors open and gestures for me to step outside.

Sun. A few moments in the open air. If Faruk weren't waiting for me in the center of the courtyard, his hands clasped behind his back, I'd relish this. Instead, I'm rooted to the spot until Zaman shoves me forward.

"Josephine," Faruk says, arching a brow, "I am not a man who likes to be kept waiting."

I glare at him as I approach. "I told you last night, I can't just manufacture a cure—"

He holds up his hand. "I am not an unreasonable man. I do, however, expect complete and immediate compliance with my orders. As you are new to my household, I will forgive this one infraction."

"Infraction?"

The strike catches me by surprise, and I fall to my hands and knees, my cheek throbbing with each beat of my heart. "Only one. No more," Faruk says sharply. "Now get up."

My entire body aches from too little activity and too many blows, but I stagger upright and straighten my shoulders.

"Better." With a sweep of his arm, he gestures to a stone wall more than twelve feet high with razor wire along the top. Four guard towers mark the corners, each with two men—AK-47s slung over their shoulders. "Before you begin treating my son, I wanted to show you some of your new home," he says with a fake smile. "I protect what is mine. Nothing and no one comes in or out without my knowledge. That," he points to a large metal door on a thick rolling track, "is the only exit."

My heart thumps so hard in my chest I worry I'm going to pass out, but I force myself to take a few deep breaths. I'm outside. In the sun. And no one's currently hurting me. But those small blessings don't make up for what I've just learned. There's no way I can escape.

"Walk with me, Josephine. There is something I would like to show you." Faruk starts to stroll away, and Zaman arches a brow at me, as if asking, *"Are you going to behave?"*

"I'm sorry, Amir Faruk," I say when I catch up to him. The soft slippers provide little protection against the rocky ground, and I wince as he spares me a brief glance. "I can't cure your son. I wish I could—"

"Choose your next words carefully, woman." We stop by a dark hole in the ground, and Zaman unrolls a long, thick rope ladder, hooks the last rung on a metal spike driven into the ground, and throws the bulk of it into the hole.

I inch backward, but Faruk stops me with a cold stare. "Your circumstances are quite good at present. They could be so much worse. Please," he says as he points to the ladder, "see for yourself."

No. Not down there.

I can't move, but when Zaman's hands clasp my shoulders, and he forces me to my knees, I start to panic. "I'll go. Just... don't push me over the edge!"

Rung by rung, I descend, wheezing, dizzy, terrified I'll lose my grip and fall to my death. I don't want to die. Even here. Trapped, afraid...I don't want to die. Tears burn my eyes, and when my feet touch bottom, Faruk orders me to let go of the ladder, and it slithers up the side, just out of my reach. All I can see is the very top of Faruk's head. I must be at least twenty feet down, and the walls are smooth, dark concrete. No hand-holds. No way to climb.

Hyperventilating, I brace my arm on the side of what might have been a well at one point, and then see the bucket next to me. An empty, dirty water bottle. The bloody handprint barely visible in the semi-darkness. The scratches on the wall. Lines. Hashes. Someone counting days. At least...shit. At least a hundred of them. *Oh God. He keeps people down here.*

"If you refuse to help Mateen," Faruk calls from high above, "you will be moved here. At night, the scorpions come out. The particular species we have in this part of the desert are not deadly, but their venom is quite painful."

"P-please," I sob, reaching for the bottom of the ladder like my life depends on it. Because I'm afraid it does. "Let me up. I'll...do whatever you want. I'll make the drug. I'll take care of Mateen."

Digging my short nails into my palms to stop myself from screaming, I wait for the sweet relief of breaking skin. But it doesn't come. I'm shaking too badly. Too weak. Too afraid.

And then the heavy rope ladder hits the top of my head. When I reach the last rung, I collapse on the rocky ground, sucking air in through my teeth and peering up at the clear, blue sky.

Zaman orders me to get up, and I push to my hands and knees, then to my feet, but still trapped in the throes of my panic attack, the world spins around me, until an arm wraps around my waist and I sink against a man who smells like incense and mint.

"Breathe," he says quietly.

The man from last night. The one Faruk ordered to erase my identity.

"Isaad!" Faruk snaps. "Step away from the woman. Now. Go back to your work."

"Do not give him reason to throw you into the hole," Isaad whispers before letting me go and hurrying around a corner to the far side of the compound.

Faruk heads back to the house, and I force myself to move, one foot in front of the other, following him until he stops in front of a room painted bright yellow.

Inside, a lab table lines one wall, complete with medical texts, notebooks, pens, and a copy of my research paper. On the other side of the room, a small bed is made up with bright blue sheets covered with soccer balls, an IV pole bolted to the headboard.

As he skims his hand over the lab bench, he looks almost proud. "This is where you will do your work. Some of the items you require are already in the refrigerator. The rest will arrive tomorrow. After midday prayers, Lisette will bring Mateen to you for a transfusion. I expect a report at the end of each day with your progress. Do you understand?"

He looms over me, his pale gray eyes cold, and I nod. "Yes...sir."

When he leaves, I sink down onto the little bed, drop my head into my hands, and let myself cry.

THE TENTATIVE KNOCK on the door startles me, and I swipe at my cheeks before I turn to see Lisette with Mateen standing at her side, his hand clutched in hers.

"You are Josephine?" she asks softly, her accent subtly different from her husband's, more musical.

"Y-yes." I meet her wary gaze. "Everyone calls me Joey."

"Lisette. This is my son, Mateen." She urges the boy forward, and he offers me a shy smile.

As horrible as my situation is, this child had no part in what's happened to me, and his feverish cheeks and pale skin tug at my heart. Dropping to my knees, I rest my hands on my thighs. "Hi, Mateen. I'm Dr. Joey. Do you speak English?"

He doesn't answer, but Lisette nods. "His father wants him to be fluent."

With a wobbly smile, I point to the portable video game system in his hand. "What games do you have on there? I used to be pretty good at Pokemon."

Mateen looks at me like I'm a relic from another time. "FIFA 19. Pokemon is for babies."

"Well, I played it a very long time ago. How about I make you a deal? I'll examine you and give you a blood transfusion so you'll feel a little better, and you can show me how to play FIFA 19. I need to learn a grown-up game if I'm going to be helping a grown-up young man like you."

"Okay." Mateen lets me lead him over to the bed and ease the video game out of his hands, and I swallow hard. I'm a doctor, and this is my patient. As scared as I am, as hopeless as my situation feels, I can help this boy. I can't cure him, but I should at least be able to stop the disease from getting worse. I just hope I can buy myself enough time to figure a way out of here before Faruk realizes a cure will never come.

"Lisette? When did Mateen first start to show symptoms?" My voice trembles, and I look over my shoulder at Lisette as I pluck a stethoscope from the lab bench.

Watery brown eyes meet mine, then dart to the ceiling in the far corner of the room for a split second before she answers. "Around his first birthday."

Shit. I was so wrapped up in my own fear, I didn't even check the room for cameras, but as I make a show of opening one of the notebooks and uncapping a pen, I flick my gaze upwards. A tiny red light glows on a black box, and when I turn back around, I see the truth in her eyes. She's as scared of Faruk as I am. And probably just as much a prisoner.

"Papa says once you fix me, I'll be as strong as he is," Mateen says with a wide smile.

I force a smile. "Yes. You will be. Just like...Papa."

6

Ford

HEFTING my go-bag over my shoulder, I follow Trevor off the transport plane outside of Qarshi, Uzbekistan. A two hour flight to Fort Bragg, North Carolina, from Boston, then nine and a half hours over the Atlantic Ocean and Europe to Kars, Turkey, then another two hour flight here.

Trevor slept. I didn't. I studied satellite images of Turkmenistan, trying to trace Joey's path east, the photos Nomar sent of the massacre he found where they were taken, and all the intel Trevor, Dax, and Wren pulled on human trafficking in the area.

Ford, I did some research in between working on Evianna's case, and most reports I can find have trafficking shipments traveling on two primary routes. Both cut right through Afghanistan. One runs just outside of Kandahar and the other west of Mazari Sharif. I found one auction site on the dark web, but so far none of the women listed there match Joey or the others with her. I'm still searching. Good luck and stay safe. - Wren

P.S. Ry's going a little stir crazy. Are you sure you don't want him and Inara to head out to meet you?

I want to say yes. To tell Wren to send Ry and let him do what he does best. But Trevor doesn't want any extra bodies around—especially not one close to seven-feet-tall with such recognizable scars and a seriously bad attitude.

As we enter the hanger, a marine private salutes us, and I return the gesture. "Staff Sergeant Ford Lawton," I say. "Retired."

"Private O'Rilley," the man says. "I got word your contact should be here in twenty minutes with a private plane. If you head to the south corner of the hanger, we've got coffee and MREs. A couple of couches. They're not comfortable, but they're yours, sirs."

With a nod, I motion for Trevor to follow me. But he's already halfway towards the makeshift office. By the time I push through the door, he's on his phone, speaking Pashto. I never learned much—and what I did has faded with the years —but his severe expression twists my gut with anxiety. I send Dax a quick message.

Ford: We're in Uzbekistan. Nomar should be here in a few minutes. I'll touch base when we get into Turkmenistan.

He doesn't respond, but the past few weeks, he's been so closed off, I'm not surprised.

After a cup of the worst coffee on the planet, I start to pace until Trev hangs up the phone. "They're not in Turkmenistan," he says, his voice grave. "They've already crossed the border into Afghanistan."

"How do you know?" I press my palms flat on the desk and loom over him. I'm a big guy—six-foot-ten—and while I'm not as bulky as Ryker, I'm solid. Trev's a good five inches shorter than I am, and he peers up at me with tired, intense eyes.

"Before we left, I sent messages to a couple of the guys I

know who are still embedded under deep cover. Told them to set up a buy for me. Western women, fresh. Age didn't matter as long as they were new to the trade."

My heartbeat thrums in my ears as my blood boils. "Watch your tone, Trev."

"You want this done fast? I'm not going to pretty up my words just because you've had a candle burning for this woman for the past twenty years. And if you lose it like this when we're with the buyers, you'll blow the whole op. So get your shit together. Understood?"

I let out a breath and back off. Easing my way down onto the well-worn sofa, I drop my head into my hands. "Sorry. Keep going."

Glancing around the room, he shakes his head, then rummages in his bag and pulls out a small metal device the size of a cigarette lighter. After he's pressed a button on the side, he continues. "Never know who's listening, and this is 'ears only.' The Turkmen border is a fucking fortress. They'll search your car license plate to license plate and run your passport through so many checks, trying to get into the White House while on a terrorist watch list is easier."

"Seriously? When did that happen?"

Trevor shrugs. "A few years ago. Does it matter?"

"Nothing matters but Joey and the other two women. Go on."

"Four vehicles passed through the checkpoints over the past few days that raise suspicion. Based on the money that changed hands when they did, one of them had drugs, another guns, and the other two were carrying people."

"And...?" Impatient for him to get to the fucking point, I dig my fingers into my thighs so I don't wrap them around his throat and shake the information out of him.

Trev runs a hand through his dark hair. "I don't know much

more than that. But there's an auction taking place in Kabul tonight. It's the only one for the next two weeks, so if they're being sold, that's where they'll be. And my contact swears there are girls available who meet my...*needs*."

"But you don't know if Joey's one of them." Defeated, I sink back against the cushions. "What if your contact's wrong? What if Joey and the other two are in Kandahar by now? Or worse... what if they *are* still in Turkmenistan?" So many possibilities run through my mind. I don't improvise. Don't take chances. That's Clive's territory. Ella's. Hell, even Dax's. Not mine.

"*Think*, Ford. Be logical. This is our best lead so far. I'm still working a dozen angles, and by the auction tonight, maybe one of them will come through. Or...we'll find them, get them the fuck out of there before they're sold, and be on a transpo home before breakfast. I know you love her, but you haven't slept and you need to get your head on straight before we get to Kabul."

I nod. He's right. He's also thirty-six and looks like a baby compared to me. But Dax and I hired him on the spot when we interviewed him. He's brilliant. Can analyze ten different outcomes in a matter of moments, then give you the run-down on pros and cons of each. Not to mention his tech skills. He's no Wren, but he's made his bones in the field.

"You have to trust me. I spent five years running between Afghanistan, Uzbekistan, and Pakistan. I know the people, the customs, and the secrets. We won't get to Kabul for at least five hours. You focus on the endgame, you understand? Sleep, and for fuck's sake, let me do my thing. It's the only way this works."

Two quick raps on the office door have us both turning in unison, and Trevor's hand goes to his hip—the guy's been packing the whole time, while my weapons are still safely stowed in my go bag.

A short, stocky man with black hair, a full beard, and ice in his blue eyes steps into the room. "Never thought I'd see you back here again, Moana."

"Nomar." The tension between them could cut glass, and I push to my feet.

"You know each other?" I ask.

Trevor snorts. "You could say that."

With a small shake of his head, Nomar grabs my hand and pulls me in for a one-armed hug. "Good to see you again, Ford. Sorry it's under these circumstances. If we're going to make Kabul before the air traffic controllers I bribed go off shift, we need to head out right now. Grab your gear." He turns on his heel and strides back through the door, Trevor following too quickly for me to ask him what the fuck just happened.

But as soon as I'm buckled into the jump seat on a plane that looks more like a toy than anything else, I give them both a hard stare. "I don't know what's up between the two of you, but if you let it affect this mission—"

"Classified," both men say at once.

Trevor turns and clamps a hand down on my shoulder as Nomar pulls on his ear protection and starts flipping switches and levers, the plane's engines roaring to life. "We're all on the same side, Ford. I don't have to like the guy to work with him. It's enough that I respect his skills."

"Agreed," Nomar says. "What happened in Qatar...stays there. All that matters now is getting Joey back."

I relax against the seat and close my eyes. Trev's right. I'm no good to anyone if I can't think straight. The three of us are going to have a serious talk before this is all over, but right now, I need to rest so I'm on top of my game. Joey needs me.

Joey

My eyelids feel like sandpaper, and my stomach does somersaults as I stand in front of Faruk to report on my progress.

"Mateen's anemia is much better, but the more transfusions I give him, the higher his iron levels are going to be. I need a way to chelate his blood. Until he's stable for at least a week, I won't be able to even guess at the amounts of the various drugs in the cocktail to give him."

"You are stalling, Josephine." Faruk arches a brow, approaching with his hands clasped behind his back. I drop my gaze, fighting my urge to bolt. He doesn't seem like the type of man to get his hands dirty, and Zaman looms behind me. "Would you like to spend a few nights in the hole?"

"N-no, please." Shrinking away from him, I hug myself tightly. "If I start him on the cocktail now...he could die. The final components only came in this morning. I...can show you my notes. All my calculations. I wrote that paper seven years ago. Two of the drugs have had formula changes since then. I have to redo all of my testing to make sure they won't kill him."

"Excuses." Faruk shakes his head and waves Zaman over.

I can't let them take me to that dark hole. I'll never survive a night there. Straightening my shoulders and rooting my feet to the floor, I raise my head and stare Faruk in his stormy gray eyes. "If I rush this process, Mateen will suffer—he could even die. He's a smart boy. A good boy. And he's *my* patient. I may hate you and what you've done to bring me here, but I *will* treat him. I haven't stopped...haven't taken a break. You should know. You're watching me every minute. I made a lot of progress today, but I won't risk his life if I'm not 100% positive the cocktail is safe."

For several long minutes, we stare at one another. I can't hear anything but my own heartbeat roaring in my ears. Have I just sealed my own fate? Or bought myself another few days?

"You have much to learn about respect, Josephine," Faruk says, and Zaman tightens his hands around my upper arms, giving me a hard shake. He's pressed to my back, and I want to throw up, but I'm too terrified with Faruk only two feet away. "The next time you speak to me that way, you will spend a night in the hole. Zaman, take her back to her room."

I'm so relieved, I don't even realize until I'm locked in that I never got lunch or dinner.

7

Ford

THE DIM LIGHTS and dark corners set my nerves on edge as Trev and I follow a pair of heavily armed men through a crowded restaurant on the western edge of Kabul. It's a little after seven —prime dinner hour—but the restaurant is a known front for all kinds of illegal activity. Drugs, guns...and flesh.

"Remember, let me do the talking," Trevor whispers. "You'll just get us all killed."

"Your confidence in me is inspiring." He's probably not wrong. Despite catching an hour of sleep on the plane and another three hours at a tiny CIA safehouse in the middle of the city, I know I'm not at my best.

"Ford—"

"I know." Tugging at the loose charcoal jacket over the black t-shirt, I tamp down the urge to remind him I'm technically his boss. Here, he's in charge, and I'm the grunt doing what I'm told. We dressed the parts. His suit cost double what mine did.

"You have the cash?" one of the AK-47 wielding goons asks as he rests his hand on a biometric keypad. A green light scans his palm, then the lock clicks open, but he doesn't move to let us through.

Trevor shows the man his phone with evidence of two million dollars in an offshore account. The money's fake, but they won't be able to confirm that until we're well out of here—we hope. "This enough?" he asks, adopting an accent that sounds completely local.

The big guy grunts his agreement and heads down a long hall, and before the door shuts behind us, sealing off the restaurant from what happens in the secret back rooms, I catch a glimpse of Nomar passing by one of the side windows. If all goes well, his diversion will give us the chance to get out of there at the end of the auction with Joey, Mia, and Ivy. Assuming they're even here.

Another door and another palm scanner lead to a small, sparse room. My heart stops. Against the far wall, five women are lined up, flanked by two men with AK-47s held at the ready. Joey isn't one of them.

They're all wearing white or black negligées, their wrists shackled together in front of them, with metal collars around their necks. Each collar connects to the next with a heavy chain, ensuring none of them can run without the others.

Ivy's first, with Mia last, though I barely recognize them. They looked so fresh-faced and innocent in their passport photos. Now...their eyes are glassy, their cheeks sunken, and they've lost weight. A lot of it.

Mia's forearm arm is encased in a heavy cast, and her body bears dozens of deep, dark bruises. All of them look defeated, terrified, but Ivy, one of only two wearing white, is largely unmarked—only deep purple finger marks around her upper arms and ligature burns around her ankles.

Men gather in front of the girls, a few of them whispering to one another. Most are older, dressed in the finest suits—both Western and traditional.

"She's not here," I whisper.

Over comms, Nomar's voice is low and gravely. "Ready when you are."

"Wait for my signal," Trevor says under his breath as he heads over to the rest of the buyers and starts to scan the line of women. Pausing in front of Mia, he jerks his head towards the closest guard. "This one is damaged."

The man grumbles something I don't understand, and Trevor fakes a laugh. "I like a little spirit in my harem."

A dark-haired man dressed in a white suit slips out from behind another door. "Gentlemen, if you will take your seats, we will begin. I am your host, Mr. Black. Tonight, there are five pieces of merchandise up for sale. Payment will be due immediately after the final auction. For those of you without secure transport, delivery can be arranged for a nominal fee."

Digging my fingers into my thighs as I sit down, I keep my gaze on Ivy. We have to get them out of here and pray they know where Joey is.

Next to the women, the auctioneer clears his throat and gestures to Ivy. "The first piece is twenty-three, one-hundred-sixty-two centimeters tall, and weighs forty-five kilograms. Black hair, green eyes. She is untouched, so the bidding will start at fifty thousand American dollars."

Four of the men get into a bidding war over her, and Trevor leans over to whisper in my ear as tears stream down Ivy's porcelain cheeks. "She'll fetch the highest price of the night as a virgin. But that also means they won't have raped her already." As he straightens, he holds up his hand. "One hundred and fifty thousand."

By the time the Trevor's outbid the other four men, Ivy's price is well over two hundred thousand. "Sold. This next item is seventeen, one-hundred-forty centimeters tall, and weighs thirty-nine kilograms. Bidding starts at thirty thousand dollars."

This girl looks like she came straight from one of the local villages, and she's terrified, sobbing and shaking as a final price is agreed upon. Mia's last, and after the auctioneer reads her vital statistics, he nods towards her arm. "She was damaged during transport, but this will not hinder her use. Bidding begins at twenty-thousand."

Mia glares at the asshole like she wants to rip his dick off and shove it down his throat.

Trevor once again outbids every other man in the room—though Mia's final price is less than fifty thousand. And then... it's over.

The elbow to my ribs startles me, and Trevor jerks his head towards the women. The guards are unlocking the chains connecting their collars in preparation for handing them off to their buyers. "Time to go." Lowering his voice, he mutters, "On my mark."

Like a good bodyguard, I trail behind him. The goons outside scanned us for metal before they let us in the restaurant, but I have a ceramic knife tucked into my boot and Trevor's belt turns into at least three separate weapons. Fucking spook has all the good toys.

Trevor strides up to Mr. Black with an air of impatience plastered across his face. "I have a plane leaving in under an hour. Remove their wrist cuffs and cover them. I will not have others looking at what is now mine."

Mr. Black nods at the guards who each pull out a set of keys and start removing the handcuffs. Ivy and Mia immediately move towards one another, Ivy's arm wrapping around Mia's shoulders. "Of course. If you will transfer payment—"

"Now," Trevor barks, and the rafters shake as the small explosion rattles the building. Bits of dust and plaster rain down, the girls start to scream, and Trevor and I spring into action.

The guards try to round up the women, but I drop and roll,

coming up with the knife in my hand. With a quick jab, I sink the ceramic blade into the closest guard's side, twist, and drop him where he stands.

Trevor pulls off his belt, twists the buckle, and pulls taut, exposing a thin, metal wire. A shot whizzes by my ear, and I spin, aiming a kick to Mr. Black's solar plexus as Trevor dispatches the second armed man.

But in the next breath, three others race in from a side door. Trevor goes for Black, and I grab a gun off the floor, firing twice, dropping two of the three new assholes. The third grabs Ivy, but she wriggles and kicks until her fist finds his balls, and he drops her.

Another shot makes us all spin around to see Nomar in the doorway, his gun drawn and a look of murderous rage in his eyes. The man who'd grabbed Ivy is gurgling on the floor, blood filling his lungs. He won't live another five minutes.

Tucking the gun back into his holster, Nomar grabs one of the sets of keys from the closest guard and starts to unlock the other women's shackled wrists.

"You want to live?" Trevor asks, and Mr. Black starts to choke and wheeze as the garrote bites into his neck. "Where's Josephine Taylor?"

"J-Joey?" Ivy stammers. "She...they separated us. Days ago."

"Where is she?" Trevor asks again, pulling the wire even tighter.

"Not...here," Mr. Black wheezes, his fingers desperately trying to loosen the wire, to no avail. "She...was...never to be...sold."

Taking my knife, I cut through the waistband of his pants, his briefs, and expose his flaccid cock. "If you ever want to be able to use this pathetic dick again, you'll tell us where she is."

"Amir Abdul Faruk. He has her. The other two," he gestures weakly towards Ivy and Mia, "were not part of his plan, so he had his men bring them to me." His shoulders sag.

"He will kill me if I do not deliver his money tomorrow. Please..."

Trevor meets my gaze. We have a way in. "I'm going to kill you anyway," Trev whispers in the man's ear, and as Mr. Black whimpers pathetically, I turn to Nomar.

"Come on. We have to get out of here," I say, not wanting the women to witness yet another death. Nomar translates for the three who look like they could be locals, ushering them out the door to the waiting van, and I extend my hand to Ivy, who still holds Mia tightly.

The two share a look, then Mia straightens in Ivy's embrace and they both stare expectantly at Mr. Black. "If you're going to kill him," Mia says, her voice hoarse and weak, "we're going to watch."

"Are you sure?" They look so fragile, but then again, I can understand their need to see the man who hurt them die.

"Yes," they answer in unison.

Trevor pulls the garrote tight, and Mr. Black's face turns purple, then blue as he bucks and thrashes with his last breaths. Blood seeps around the wire, then pours freely from his carotid artery, and with a final muttered curse, Trevor lets him go where he falls to the floor, his eyes open and staring.

Mia sobs quietly, but Ivy pins me with a hard stare. "Who are you?"

"Ford Lawton. I...used to know Joey. A long time ago. Can we save the rest of the explanation for the van?"

"Hell, yeah." Ivy urges Mia towards the door, and once we're in the van racing towards the safehouse, Ivy touches my arm. "Ford?" Her shoulders are straighter and her eyes hold a fire I didn't see when she was chained and about to be sold. "Joey's strong. She tried to protect us—until they came and took the two of us away."

"Where were you?"

"I don't know. But they put us in this tiny little compartment

—almost like a coffin—in the back of a van, and it was hours before they let us out again."

From the front seat, Nomar says, "That's how they got you over the border."

"Did you ever hear the name Mr. Black mentioned?" I ask. "Amir Abdul Faruk?"

"A couple of times," Mia whispers. "He was in charge of the guys who transported us. They kept saying how much Ivy would go for." She shudders and turns her cheek into Ivy's neck, her next words muffled. "I wasn't as valuable. So... they...they..."

"It's okay," I say softly. "You're both safe now. I promise. This is Trevor, and that grump behind the wheel is Nomar. We're all ex-military or US Intelligence. We'll get you home. All of you. And we're not leaving Joey behind. We'll find her."

8

Ford

A LITTLE AFTER 11:00 p.m., one of Nomar's contacts, a Brit named Matthew, knocks on the safehouse door. He—along with three of his most trusted agents—will protect Ivy, Mia, and the other girls until we can make arrangements to get them all home to their families.

"Matt," Nomar says as he claps the tall, thin man on the back. "Thanks for this."

"You saved my arse, mate. I've been trying to put an end to that bastard's trafficking ring for three years. But he's always smelled a rat before we got in there." Behind him, two other men and one woman wait for Matt to introduce them.

"Ford?" Ivy asks from the bedroom door. "Is everything okay?" She holds a blanket tightly around her and darts a glance back at the bed where Mia sleeps. She passed out almost as soon as her head hit the pillow.

"Just fine, sweetheart. Matt and his team are going to stay with you until we find Joey and can get the hell out of here," I say.

The woman with Matt steps forward and holds out a duffel bag. "I brought clothes—various sizes. Sweats, long sleeves, socks. And some fancy shampoo and soap. I'm Tara," she says with a smile. "You're Ivy?"

Ivy nods, but pushes past Tara and grabs my arm. "You have to find her, Ford. Please. Joey took care of us. The three weeks we were in Turkmenistan working? She was the one who taught us how to make the locals feel comfortable. How to double-check the tent frames to make sure they were solid. How to sleep at night when it was so hot."

I arch a brow, and Ivy offers me a weak smile. "Put on fresh socks."

"That sounds like Joey. She was always so practical. And she never let anyone struggle if she could help it. We'll get her back." I don't finish my sentence, but the words echo in my head. *Or die trying.*

———

THE JEEP BOUNCES OVER rutted roads, jostling me awake. One thing you learn in the military? How to grab small bits of sleep here and there. Whenever you can. The past five hours, I've proved how much I still know.

"Finally awake? Thank God. You were starting to drool," Trevor says from the front seat. With a glare, I swipe my hand over my mouth, only to find it dry as a bone. Jerk.

Darkness still holds sway over the sky, but a hint of light brightens the horizon in the east. Still, the stars shine this far from any major city. Checking my GPS, I sit up with a start. We're not far outside of Mazari Sharif. Less than twenty minutes from where we *think* they're holding Joey.

"Any news?" There's no cell service here, but if I know Trevor, he's been on and off his SAT phone the entire five hour drive.

"Maybe. Amir Abdul Faruk has been on the terrorist watch list for seven years," Nomar says. He nods at Trevor, and the former spook passes me a tablet. On screen, a man stands outside a massive home surrounded by a tall, stone wall. Next to him, a smaller figure—a woman—dressed in burnt orange, and behind her, another man. Stockier. With something that looks vaguely like a gun. The time stamp reads two days ago.

"This is the best you got?" I ask, trying to zoom in. If this is Joey...

"The satellite only passes over this region once every forty-eight hours—usually. But we got it retasked to keep a constant watch until we know if she's really there," Nomar says. "If she goes outside again, we'll get a better shot."

"Do I want to know how many favors you called in to commandeer a satellite?"

"No," he and Trevor answer at once, then share a chuckle. While I slept, they must have worked out some of their shit.

Trevor turns in the front seat and meets my gaze. "Faruk is a paranoid fucknut. There are guards at each corner of that wall with AK-47s. One way in and out—the gate. Razor wire every-where else. This isn't going to be easy."

"I can call Ryker, but it'll take him at least twenty-four hours to get his team here."

"No." Running his hand through his dark hair, Trevor frowns. "Look, I know the guy's K&R. And it might come to that eventually. But we're breaking so many laws, they could put us all away for the rest of our fucking lives if we're caught."

He meets my gaze, and I understand. He's doing this for Wren. Keeping *her* safe by keeping the man she loves safe. And I can't blame him. But this is Joey. I won't lose her. I can't. "Let me call him. At least tell him to stand by. Put his team on notice. Send him some of this intel. We don't know what this Faruk is doing to Joey. Or how long she has left."

With a grumbled response that might be a "fine," he turns back to the road.

"Ford?" Nomar and I lock eyes in the rearview. "This isn't like when we were deployed. There were rules there. Even with Saddam as batshit as he was. This is rural Afghanistan. And most of this area? It was a Taliban hotbed for years. The locals won't be any help. They'll actively try to kill us."

And Joey.

"If you're saying we shouldn't rescue her—" My entire body vibrates with anger, and Nomar's lucky he's driving.

"Whoa, there. Nobody's saying that. I wouldn't leave a woman I *hated* in that situation, let alone one I cared for. But you haven't been 'in country' for more than a dozen years. We have. And I need your guarantee you'll follow our lead."

I must have missed a hell of a lot of conversation while I was napping. "Trev and I already had this talk. Why are we rehashing it again?"

"Because I put in my retirement papers a month ago. When you called, I was wiping my apartment clean. Twenty minutes later, and I would have been gone. Headed back to the States. Everything we're doing...we don't have any sort of official support. I'm a civvie now. Just like you. And I'd rather not spend the rest of my life in an Afghan prison. Or...without my head if they find out we killed all those assholes at the auction."

Shit.

NOMAR EASES the Jeep off the road and down a little hill to a group of tents as the dawn threatens to spill over the horizon. "These guys owe me. They'll hide the Jeep and give us horses. We'll never get a vehicle closer to the compound than this without being shot."

Nothing said in the next ten minutes makes any sense to

me. Trevor, Nomar, and two older Afghan men gesture and argue, until finally, another man brings out three tunics for us to put on over our fatigues and black t-shirts.

The horses look just as thrilled to be saddled up this early in the morning as I feel relying on an animal—one that can't outrun a car—for our only transportation. But Trevor's right. If we try to take the Jeep any closer, Faruk's men will see and hear us coming, and that could be deadly—for us and for Joey.

"Good news," Trevor says as we mount up and urge the horses forward. "One of Faruk's men is...*dissatisfied* with the way the asshole runs things. He'll get Nomar into the compound for the right price."

"And what's the right price?" I don't really want to know, but after working with Dax for the past few years, I've socked away a nice nest egg. Private security work pays well.

"Ten grand." With a shrug, he lets Nomar get twenty or thirty feet in front of us before lowering his voice. "Dax is funding this whole thing up to six figures. After that—"

"What?" Telling me the sky was made of horse shit wouldn't have surprised me this much. A hundred thousand dollars? Money he clearly didn't think twice about since he didn't bother to mention it to me.

"The dude's loaded." Trevor arches a brow. "You didn't know? Jesus, Ford. Look at how he lives. That tiny apartment? No car, no parking fees or insurance. He hasn't taken a single day off since you two hired me. Who does that?"

"Dax." I shake my head with a sigh. "When we get back, he and I are going to have a serious talk about work-life balance."

"Like you're much better."

"What's that supposed to mean? I leave the office by six most nights."

"And do what? Go home? Watch baseball? Read a book?" He shoots me a pointed look. "When's the last time you got laid?"

"*This* is the conversation you want to have right now?"

"Yes." His tone turns grave. "Because we're about to go try to rescue a woman you haven't seen in twenty years, and every time one of us says her name, the look on your face? You're still in love with her. Tell me I'm wrong."

"I can't." Transferring the reins to one hand, I scrub the other over my eyes for a brief moment. "I've loved Joey all my life. Tried to date on and off. Never lasted longer than a month. None of them measured up." As I dig my heels into the horse's sides and urge him to pick up the pace, I admit the truth to Trevor—and maybe to myself. "Joey was it for me. *Is* it for me. I have to tell her, Trev. Whatever happens after that...she needs to know I never stopped loving her."

BY THE TIME we tie the reins to a post behind an abandoned barn at the bottom of the hill, my legs are on fire and my ass is numb. "I really don't like horses," I mutter as we drop our rucksacks.

The sun starts to brighten the sky, silhouetting the wall and the four stories of stone and clay that make up Faruk's compound. Nomar obsessively checks and rechecks the gun strapped to his side under his tunic. I don't like this plan, but it's all we have. I can't just waltz up to Faruk's front gate and ask him to hand over the woman he kidnapped.

The village hasn't stirred, the only sounds the goats and chickens wandering the paths between small houses. Roads would be too generous of a term. There isn't a single vehicle in sight, only horses tied to posts, a few of them neighing quietly, but most still sleeping.

Nomar rummages in his sack, pulls out a headscarf and an AK-47, checks his pistol one last time, and starts toward the compound's gate.

The comms unit in my ear clicks once, and then his voice whispers over the connection. "There's a small camera hidden in one of the buttons on this getup. But the range sucks. You'll have to be close. Make your way to the back of the compound, and for fuck's sake, stay out of sight. I'll get in, find out where they're holding her, and get out. Do *not* engage unless there's no other way. Got it?"

"Got it," I say. Meeting Trevor's gaze, I offer a silent prayer Nomar will find her alive, then follow the spook to the outskirts of the village, climb the hill towards the back of the compound, and wait.

Joey

Jerking awake from yet another nightmare, I reach for the ring hidden under my tunic. I'm so tired, but I can't relax. Can't manage to sleep for more than half an hour at a time. Mateen is a bright, kind boy. Every day after I take his blood and give him the various supplements and medications that will prepare his body for the final cocktail, he tells me about some famous soccer player he wants to meet or challenges me to a match on his little gaming system.

But his father...his father will soon turn him into a monster. I see the fear in Lisette's eyes every time Faruk comes to check on the boy. When he was finished with his treatment yesterday, Mateen wanted to stay with his mother, but Faruk refused to allow it.

At least then, I was left alone in the makeshift lab. More or less. The camera watches me incessantly, and Zaman often hovers in the doorway. And tonight...I'll have to tell Faruk the first component of the cocktail is done. How long until he forces me to start a treatment I know will kill my patient? Days?

A week at most. And then...I'll be dead too. I can't harm that little boy. If I can't figure a way out of this, I'll use the cocktail on myself. Die on my own terms and let Mateen live—for as long as his disease allows.

Pulling the tiny needle I stole out of the hem of my tunic, I open a small cut on my inner arm. The pain eases the fear I'll implode and lets me breathe again.

Lying with my back against the door, fully dressed, save for my headscarf and slippers, I try to call up a single happy memory. Anything to hold on to.

"Oh, crap. I'm so sorry," I cry as my soda tumbles down the shirt of the most delicious, handsome man I've ever seen. "I wasn't watching where I was going." Turning back to the counter, I grab wads and wads of napkins, then try to soak up the icy liquid from a strong chest until I realize what I'm doing. My hands are all over him.

With flushed cheeks, I step back, staring down at the floor. "Can I...um...buy you...another... Oh, I hope you weren't on your way somewhere important."

"Just lunch. Alone," he says. "Though I was hoping to drink soda rather than wear it."

The smile in his voice encourages me enough to meet his gaze, and...wow. Hazel eyes flecked with green. Strong cheekbones. A little bit of a light brown scruff dusting his chin. And that grin. That full bottom lip.

"Coca-Cola brown is a good color on you."

The man laughs, and my God if that doesn't make him even more handsome. "Ford," he says, holding out his hand.

As our fingers brush, a spark races up my arm, quickening my heartbeat. "Josephine. Joey."

Playing the memory like a movie on repeat, I close my eyes, run my fingers over the ring I never could force myself to send back to him, and pray this time when I drift off, I'll dream of a time I felt...normal.

THE DOOR SWINGS OPEN, and Zaman's boot connects with my back a moment before he falls, landing on his hands and knees, his big body pressing down on me. I scream, the last vestiges of my nightmare melding with my reality, and start to thrash and claw at him.

"Get off me! Get off! Oh, God. Please!"

Zaman grunts and pushes to his feet. "Up. Now. You are needed."

His words barely register, and I scramble back until I hit the bed. "Don't touch me!"

As if he'd listen. Grabbing my arm, he drags me to my feet and then shoves the headscarf at me. "Cover yourself."

My hands shake as I tuck the scarf around my hair and slide my feet into the slippers. He curls his thick fingers around my bicep and pulls me down the hall, up the stairs, and out into the courtyard. On a prayer mat, Mateen moans softly while Lisette kneels next to him, smoothing his hair.

Faruk looms over both of them, and when he sees me, he strides over and slaps me across the face. "You are making him worse, not better!"

"No!" I cry. "All of his numbers were better last night. You saw the report!"

Shoving me to the ground, Faruk grabs the back of my neck and holds my head close to the boy. "Does he look better to you? He fell over during morning prayers and he will not get up."

The pressure of his grip makes me tremble. He could snap my neck in a heartbeat. But I check Mateen's pulse, then palpate his belly and his lymph nodes. "It's just barely sunrise," I say, unable to keep the harsh edge from my voice. "He needs to rest. He shouldn't be up this early. And what did he eat for dinner last night?"

"My son will be with me for prayers. Always. He ate the same as the rest of the men. Liver kebabs and lentil stew."

Jerking out of Faruk's grip, I glare up at him. "I told you he needed fresh fruits and vegetables, bland food, and only the bare minimum of meat. Liver? It's full of iron—something he does *not* need more of. You just set him back weeks!"

The kick to my stomach makes me retch, and I double over, desperate to catch my breath and keep down whatever's left of the few bites of dinner I managed to eat last night. Curling into a ball, I absorb the blows to my back, his fists landing time and time again, until a man's voice calls out, "Amir Faruk, sir. The doctor cannot cure your son if you...break her."

When Faruk steps back, panting, I risk peeking up at the other man. Isaad. Every time I see him, I'm more and more certain that he's not Middle Eastern. Once in a while, he almost sounds like he's from Texas. Blue eyes stare down at me, something uncertain swimming in his gaze. With a barely imperceptible nod, I thank him for saving me, though I'm not sure whether he's truly done so or just given me a stay of execution.

"Take her to the lab along with my son," Faruk grits out. As Zaman drags me along the ground by the back of my tunic, my captor spits in my direction. "I expect my son to join me for prayers by nightfall, Josephine. If he does not, I will hold you responsible."

9

Ford

IT TAKES everything I have in me to sit, unmoving, as Nomar's camera broadcasts that asshole kicking and punching Joey as she curls into a ball on the ground. But, she's alive. And before he started in on her, she looked almost defiant. Strong. He hasn't broken her yet.

One man drags Joey back inside and another picks up Faruk's son. His wife, Lisette, a French national whose parents reported her missing ten years ago, trails after them, swiping at her cheeks.

Faruk and another man head for the other side of the courtyard, and Nomar whispers, "I'm going to try to find out where they took Joey."

On the tablet screen in Trevor's hands, the shaky video shows hallways, plush rugs, antiques, and heavy draperies. The signal cuts out when he starts down a narrow stairwell, and Trev switches to tracking Nomar's GPS signal. A small, red dot moves within the outlines of the compound, pausing here and there, occasionally speeding up. Clenching my hands hard enough to leave bruises, I replay the whole scene in my head over and over again.

Joey being dragged outside, the way she immediately focused on the boy, checked on him, protected him.

"Do we have any intel on Faruk's son?" I whisper. "Joey's a big deal in pediatric medicine, and that kid looked pretty sick. He's what? Seven? Eight?"

With a glare, Trevor warns me to be quiet, then points up at the guards in the tower fifty feet away. If we can't get in there soon, I'm going to implode.

Over comms, Nomar's harsh whisper sets me on edge. "I found her. The kid's hooked up to an IV. I couldn't stick around. Guards and cameras all around here. Give me twenty minutes to map the rest of the place, then I'll meet you back at the barn. We'll infiltrate tonight."

Hunching over the tablet, I try to hunt and peck my way through the massive file Trev compiled on Amir Abdul Faruk. "His son has something called thalassemia. He's been in the hospital in Kabul four times in the past two years."

Trevor runs a hand through his hair and then tugs at his black tunic. "I hate this fucking thing. When I quit the CIA, I swore I'd never set foot in this country again."

"I can't pay you back for this, man."

He shakes his head and takes a swig from his canteen. "Second Sight is a family, Ford. You told me that when you hired me. I know I haven't exactly been the best member of that family, sticking to myself, staying away from social hours and company events, but that doesn't mean I don't care. We don't abandon one another. And your Joey looks like a fighter. If we can get her out alive...I think she'll be okay."

"I hope so." The truth hits me hard, and I sink down on an

old crate. I don't know her at all anymore. Is she as strong as she looked this morning? Or on the verge of shattering into pieces? "The last time I talked to her, she said we'd never survive if I didn't trust her. And because I was such a dumbfuck, I didn't listen. After that...she went through some shit. It was bad, Trev. Worse than...well, anything I could imagine. It changed her. In a way I couldn't understand. Or she didn't think I could understand. Hell, she was probably right."

"Sounds like a fighter to me." Trevor pulls up the footage from Nomar's camera and taps the tablet screen. Zooming in on Joey's face, he stops the playback when she glares up at Faruk. "Look at her, Ford. She's scared. But she's not backing down."

The video quality isn't the best, but he's right. Her shoulders are thrown back and her hands clenched at her sides.

Nomar knocks twice at the barn door, then slips inside. "That place is a fucking fortress. There are cameras in every hallway, one in the room where Joey was treating the kid, and I counted twenty-two other guards. No idea how many stay on at night, but this isn't going to be easy."

I swallow hard. "I can call Ryker, but he won't be here until tomorrow at the earliest."

"Not only that," Nomar says, "but he'd probably go in there guns blazing."

"You have a better idea?"

"I do," Trevor says quietly. "But you're not going to like it."

"THE CIA HAS ALL the good toys," I mutter as I weave the high-grade plastic lock picks into the waistband of my black pants. They rest at the small of my back. In my shoe, a retractable knife the size of my little finger is embedded in the lining, and I wear the same type of belt Trevor used in Kabul.

Trevor chuckles. "You have no idea, man. All the state-of-the-art tech you can think of? The government's had it for at least three to five years longer than you'd imagine."

"You ready?" Nomar asks.

"No." Trev was right. I hate this plan. But it's also our best chance to get in and find Joey. Blowing out a single, focusing breath, I close my eyes. "Do it." Nomar's right hook catches me in the jaw, and I taste blood. The next is higher...closer to my eye. "You do realize I need to be able to see to get the fuck out of there?"

"On the ground. Got to make this look real," Trevor orders.

Sinking to my knees, I let Nomar push me into the dirt, then plant his boot in the center of my back. Trevor holds my left arm and slices through the dark brown tunic, opening up a shallow cut along my bicep. I barely notice the pain, but it'll bleed enough to look like I'm more injured than I am.

After the two men grind a little more dirt into my clothes, Nomar offers me his hand. "Thanks, asshole." I don't have to fake my groan when I get to my feet. "Let's get this over with."

I tense my muscles and angle my hands slightly as Trevor ties the rope around my wrists, tight enough to fool most people, but loose enough I can still move if I relax a bit. I'd much rather *he* be the one going in as a prisoner, but since I don't speak more than a couple of words of Pashto and Trev and Nomar do, this is the only way.

When we're almost in sight of the guard towers, Trevor takes my arm. "You trust me, right?"

I meet his gaze in the last dim light of dusk. His green eyes usually give nothing away. Training, or some damage he won't talk about, I don't know. But the guy's scary. Unnerving. I swear half the time he doesn't feel any emotion—except maybe anger. But now...? He's as worried as I am about this plan.

Bound, I can't do anything more than look him in the eyes. "I trust you with my life. But more than that, I'm trusting you with Joey's life. She's the priority. You get her out. Even if you have to leave me behind."

"Not leaving you behind," he mutters, but when I half-growl his name, he sighs. "I promise you, Ford. We'll get Joey out. No matter what."

My nod seals the vow, and he digs a hood out of his back pocket. "Look broken."

Not much of a problem there. I've been broken for twenty years. But when he shoves the dark cloth down over my head, my heart starts to pound, and my palms dampen.

By the time we reach the gate, I've fallen four different times, and my chin and knees are bleeding. Every time I trip, I curse under my breath, but we have to sell the act. I'm their prisoner and they can't show me any consideration.

A harsh voice calls out from just in front of me, and Nomar answers back in Pashto. Trevor leans in and whispers, "He's asking what business we have here."

After a few minutes of angry negotiations, metal screeches, and I'm tugged forward. I trip once more on the metal tracks, and this time, stronger, rougher hands yank me up. Not Trev or Nomar.

"You think you can steal from Amir Faruk? That auction brought in hundreds of thousands of American dollars every month. You will learn the meaning of pain for killing our men."

Something hard impacts my skull, and the darkness behind the hood turns soft before I fade away completely.

My shoulders ache, and the pain in my wrists snaps me to full awareness. With my arms stretched above my head, so tight that my boots barely touch the floor, even if they didn't find my hidden tools and weapons, I won't be able to use them.

Bright lights shine in my face, and with a groan, I raise my head and squint, hoping Nomar's around here somewhere.

"Hey, fucker. Show your face," I grunt as breathing registers from behind the lights. A dark shadow moves slowly, as if sizing me up. "I don't know what those assholes told you, but I'm innocent. I was just walking by this restaurant in Kabul when the place went crazy."

"According to my sources," the refined, accented voice says as a knife presses to my windpipe, "you not only set the explosion, but killed several of my men—including Aazar."

"I don't...know...who the fuck...that is." The blade makes it hard to swallow, and panic sets in. I can't let myself thrash or even move. I'll end up with my throat slit.

"He used the name Mr. Black in public. Perhaps that will help your memory?"

"Nope. Never...heard of him." I can almost see his face, he's so close, but my vision's still a little blurry. Blinking hard, I try to focus. Faruk.

"I should cut your throat as you cut his."

"I'd...prefer...not. Kind of like...living." I can't move my head back any further that it already is, but the knife vanishes, and a punch to my side drives the air from my lungs.

"You are American."

"Sort of. Haven't been back since '03." I try to keep sight of the haloed outline of the man moving in front of me, but my head is pounding, and the stress position strains my breathing. "Listen...cut me down. I was just looking for an open restaurant. My wife's pregnant with our fourth kid, and she was having these killer cravings. My mother-in-law made me go out to find her some shit called Bolani."

"Your wife and children...they are in Afghanistan?" I've piqued his interest now—or at least given him something he can verify. Assuming any of it were true.

"If they...weren't...would I have...been going out...for food, asshole? Seven people in a two bedroom apartment." Adding another groan for emphasis, I try to push up on my toes to relieve the pressure in my wrists. "Please, man. I didn't do anything. Let me sit down."

"Address," he snaps. "Of your family."

"Hell no." Another punch to the gut is followed quickly by a kick to the backs of my knees, and my wrists take all my weight, the metal cuffs cutting into my skin.

"I can do this all night, infidel."

I get my feet under me and straighten as much as I can. "So...can...I. Your...sources are...wrong, fuckwit. I protect my family."

"My *sources* do not lie." An alarm, like something on a watch, beeps, and Faruk sighs. "Perhaps a few hours thinking about your predicament will leave you more willing to talk." His footsteps echo on the stone floors, the lights go out, and a heavy door slams shut.

Shit. This wasn't the plan. And bound like this, I don't know how the hell I'm going to get out of here.

10

Joey

MATEEN'S EYES WIDEN, and he calls out, "Papa!" Less than a breath later, Faruk's presence registers at my back, and I jerk, whirling around to face him and knocking over the little tray of equipment next to me.

"Is my son ready for prayers?" he asks. Before I can answer, he focuses on the bruises covering Mateen's arms and chest. "What have you done to him?" He stalks closer, forcing me up against the wall, his gray eyes blazing.

"N-nothing! His treatment...requires multiple IVs. And the medications I've started him on can be hard on the veins. He *needs* to be in a hospital. They could insert a central line. It would make all these repeated IVs and injections so much easier. Less bruising." I can't move. Fear keeps my muscles locked. "Less...pain," I wheeze.

Faruk looks over at his son. "Did she hurt you?"

The boy's eyes widen, and he shakes his head. "No, Papa. Dr. Joey tells me funny stories every time she gives me medicine. Look!" He pokes at one of the darkened patches of skin and smiles. "It doesn't hurt."

"He is very...brave," I say, offering Mateen a weak smile. "He's a strong young man."

Faruk steps back, relaxing a fraction. "Very well. Come, Mateen. It is time for prayers."

"Wait!" I fumble around for a bandage with soccer balls on it, then press it to his arm where I last drew a vial of blood a few minutes ago. It's almost stopped bleeding, but the bright colors always make the kid smile. "There you are, Mateen. All done, okay?"

"Okay, Dr. Joey." He gives me a high-five and hops off the bed, then follows his father out of the room.

Lisette, seated on the other side of the bed, drops her head into her hands. "You are braver than I am. Standing up to my husband?"

With a shaky sigh, I start cleaning and resetting my instrument tray. "I don't feel brave." I glance up at the camera in the corner of the room, then lower my voice. "Mateen needs to be in a hospital, Lisette. I can keep the disease from getting worse, but I'm scared the drug cocktail won't work—or worse—that it'll kill him. And then...Faruk will kill me too."

She stifles a sob. "He will kill us all. Because Mateen is part French, there are no local matches for bone marrow. Faruk refuses to let a non-believer donate. And he blames me for my son's disease."

My heart breaks for her, and I wish I had some words of comfort I could offer. But I know she's right.

As Zaman comes into the room, I set the last instrument on the tray. The guard pulls out his notebook and inventories all of the sharp objects while I stand against the wall—his nightly routine—then orders me back to my room.

"But...I haven't eaten today," I protest when he takes my arm. "I didn't get breakfast or supper—"

"Amir Faruk says you will not eat until morning. You injured his son. This is your punishment."

I sink down onto the bed as soon as Zaman locks the door. I'm so hungry, my stomach is in knots. Faruk is reminding me that he owns me. That he controls whether I live or die. Whether I eat, have clothes, a bed, a door... Will he throw me down in that deep, dark hole next?

I suck down half a bottle of water, my gaze trained on the small bit of light seeping in from the hallway. Until the rest of the compound sleeps, I don't trust Faruk or his men not to barge in, so I won't risk a shower. Or closing my eyes even for a minute, despite how tired I am.

Carefully, I work the tiny needle free from the hem of my tunic. It's not much thicker than a couple of strands of hair, but it's enough to sting. To remind me I'm alive.

Only willing to expose a small bit of skin at my wrist, I drag the sharp point along my radial bone. The barest hint of blood wells, and a fraction of the tension seeps from my shoulders.

"You kept him alive," I whisper. "If nothing else, you gave him one more day. Gave yourself one more day." My eyes burn. One more day...for what? To huddle on the floor, terrified, while nightmares wake me every time I close my eyes, leaving me shaking, trembling with fear? To be manhandled and bruised as I'm dragged from this little prison to the makeshift lab? To be constantly threatened with the hole? With death?

The sight of Mateen's sweet face as his pain eased this morning, his high-five as he left tonight...those moments brought me joy. But they were only two small sparks in the unending darkness surrounding me.

The bruises along my back and hips ache with every breath. I worry Faruk cracked one of my ribs when he kicked me, but I won't take off my tunic to check. Because amazingly, he hasn't found the ring under my clothes yet, and without that...I fear I'd lose myself completely.

Shadows move outside my door. Footsteps too quiet to hear. Quickly, I shove the needle under the pillow and rearrange my headscarf. I won't let them see me broken. Rubbing the fresh scratch, I force my pounding heart to calm.

Tiny clicks and scrapes at the lock terrify me. This isn't Zaman. It's someone new. Backing into the far corner of the room, I flatten myself against the wall.

The man who flings open the door looks like all the others. Dressed in dark brown pants and tunic, a traditional hat largely covering his dark hair, he scans the dimly lit room. Recognition flickers in his green eyes, and he smoothes something over the locking mechanism before pulling the door almost shut behind him.

"Joey? Josephine Taylor? Come on. It's time to get out of here." His accent is decidedly American, and he holds out his hand to me. I have to be dreaming. No one would come for me. No one even knows I'm here.

"Joey? We don't have a lot of time. You need to trust me."

"Wh-who are y-you?" I take a single step forward, but when he does the same, I freeze, unable to will my limbs to move again.

"Trevor. I'm a friend." He reaches into the pocket of his tunic and pulls out a small, plastic package. As he unfurls his fingers, I gasp. "He said these might convince you."

Red Vines. A little mini-package of Red Vines. Only one person knows how much I used to love these.

"Ford? He's here? How did you—?"

"We'll explain later, Joey. Now, I need to get you out of here." Tossing me the Red Vines, he arches a brow. "We have to be quick and quiet. Are you ready?"

I clasp his hand, and for the first time since they took me, I feel something other than fear—hope. "Yes."

Trevor leads me down the hall, then stops at the bottom of the stairs. "I have the package," he whispers. "Are you on your way to Foxtrot?" After a moment, he curses under his breath. "Get your ass in gear. We only have one shot at this and we're *not* leaving a man behind." A pause, and then he shakes his head. "I know what he said, but I'm not letting that sadist have him just because you ran into 'complications.'"

Foxtrot? Is he talking about Ford? My free hand touches the ring through my tunic. I don't know how he found me, but...I want so very much to see him again.

Trevor starts up the stairs, but I stop and plant my feet. "There's only one way you could have known a package of Red Vines would get me to trust you. And Foxtrot? That's Ford. What happened to him?"

His green eyes darken, and he shakes his head. "We have to leave. Right fucking now. Faruk's men took Ford—we think to a bunker on the west side of the compound to interrogate him. But Nomar ran into 'complications' as he put it. No clue what he meant by that. Our diversion goes off in ten minutes, and if we're still here, we're dead."

Trevor tightens his grip and half-drags me through the communal dining room and back to the kitchen.

"Why is Faruk interrogating him?" I whisper as Trevor urges me to duck down so we're not seen through the window to the courtyard.

"Because we used him as leverage to get in. Said we'd caught him after he'd murdered the fucker running the flesh auction and let the girls go. His cover story is that he's an American ex-pat living in Kabul and was in the wrong place at the wrong time. But after we destroyed half the building and killed the guys running the sale, I doubt Faruk will believe him."

My heart skips a beat. "The auction? Oh God. Ivy and Mia. Are they—"

"They're safe. Now, come on. We have to get you out of here, and I'm not leaving Ford for that asshole, so you're coming with me. We just better hope no one sees us."

Readjusting my headscarf, I meet Trevor's gaze. "If we're seen, start yelling at me. Tell me how much I'll suffer. There's an old well fifty feet from the gate. That's where you say you're taking me. On Faruk's orders. Any of his men will believe it."

"Joey—"

"It'll work. Just...don't put me down there." My eyes burn, but I swallow hard as Trevor pushes through the back door and out into the night. We keep close to the wall of the house until we come across a door with a thick padlock.

Trevor pulls a small, black pouch from his pocket and crouches down. In a few seconds, the lock springs open. "I can't let you out of my sight, Joey. He'd never forgive me. Stay behind me and keep quiet."

A long set of stairs leads deep underground, and my heart thunders in my ears. The walls press in on me, and I try not to wheeze as I clench my left hand hard enough to break the skin. *Focus. Ford's here. And he needs you.*

Trevor stops at a corner, then points to the left. Flattening myself against the wall next to him, I wait for him to verify no one's waiting on the other side, then we take off at a run. His steps are almost silent. I'm not so graceful, and when he stops short, I slam into his back. My bruised ribs protest, but I manage to keep quiet.

Picking another lock with ease, he throws the door open and I clamp my hand over my mouth, tasting blood from the self-imposed cuts on my palm.

Ford.

I didn't believe—not truly. I hoped, like I've hoped for so many things these past ten days, but I didn't trust the universe not to pull the rug out from under me again. He's here. Strung up by his wrists, his head bowed, eyes closed. Older. A bit of gray in his hair. But very much Ford. Very much the man I once loved.

Trevor moves quickly, finding a chair and going to work on the shackles holding Ford up. I rush forward to try to catch him as, freed, he sinks to his knees with a soft grunt, but I'm not fast enough.

He peers up at me, one eye swollen, and I reach out, my fingers trembling, to touch his stubbly cheek. "Ford." I don't know why he doesn't touch me, but his eyes water, and what I see in their hazel depths...I never thought I'd see him look at me like that again. "Say something."

"Later," Trevor hisses. "We have to get out of here. Can you walk?"

As if he's just remembered Trevor's in the room, he blinks hard. "I'll make it."

"Lean on me," I say, desperate to feel his arms around me after so many years apart.

"Are you sure?" His whisper is so hesitant, so filled with pain, and I take his arm and sling it around my shoulders. He's a solid mass of muscle, and Trevor has to help him stand, but once he's upright, he steadies.

"Nomar's blown. Something about a complication he couldn't ignore. We're headed for the front gate. The bomb's set to go off in six minutes. Can you shoot?" Trevor asks Ford.

He turns his gaze to me. "I can do anything. Now."

As soon as Trevor presses a gun into Ford's hand, we take off, and the warmth of the man at my side feels so reassuring, I want to cry. But I can't. Not until we get out of here. Faruk has so many men...so much firepower, I don't know how they're planning on getting beyond the gate without us all being shot.

But they got in here. Maybe we can get out.

As if Ford can read my mind, he gives my shoulder a gentle squeeze. "I found you, buttercup. We're going to be okay."

"Stop," a deep voice says as a shadow crosses our path.

Trevor raises his gun. "Don't move," he growls.

Hands in the air, Isaad lowers his gaze. "I am no threat to you, but you cannot go this way. I monitor the cameras, and if I wait more than fifteen minutes to report a glitch in the feeds, he will...hurt me. Your other man is headed for the front gate, but there are too many guards between here and there. Come with me. There is an underground tunnel that leads out of the compound."

"Fuck, no," Trevor says and lunges for Isaad. But the guard sidesteps him, backing away with his hands still in the air.

"Please," Isaad says. "Let me try to atone for my sins."

"For your sins?" Ford straightens slightly, winces, and tightens his arm around my shoulder. "Your accent...you're American, aren't you? Isaad? Isaad what?"

Shouts come from the opposite side of the compound, and Trevor grabs my other arm. "We have to go. Now."

"Wait!" Isaad hisses. "The doctor is wearing a tracking device."

My entire body goes rigid as terror floods my system. "What? Where?"

"In the hem of your pants. He trusts no one. Not even his own men. Not even his wife."

Trevor crouches and runs his fingers around the bottom of both of my legs. Yanking a knife from his pocket, he rips through the thin fabric and comes up with a small piece of plastic and metal the size of my thumbnail. "Shit," he says as he drops the tracker then stomps on it and pins Isaad with a hard stare. "Why tell us?"

"Faruk took my name. And my honor. Let me earn a piece of it back." Isaad drops to his knees and bows his head with his hand over his heart. "I will kill him for what he has done. Then...maybe my ledger won't be so full of blood."

Trevor and Ford exchange a glance, then Trevor mutters something I can't make out under his breath. "Get up. Show us this tunnel. But if you're lying to us, I'm putting a bullet in each of your kneecaps before I shoot you in the head."

Isaad nods, then gestures for us to follow him through the dark shadows to the back of the compound until he comes to a wooden trapdoor. "The tunnel leads under the wall. I will give you a two-minute head start, and then I will send the guards to the east wall. After that, I will have to tell Faruk the doctor is gone and the cameras were shut down. And if I am lucky, I will be able to kill him before he kills me."

Trevor nods at Isaad, and I whisper, "Thank you."

11

Ford

JOEY WAITS for me to climb the ladder, then guides my arm back around her shoulders and lets me lean on her again. Just ahead of us, Trevor mutters, "Blow it and get out."

Five seconds later, an explosion shatters the air. Joey jerks against me, and I pull her closer as we start to run down the hill. She winces more than once, tension pulsing through her muscles every few steps, and I glance down at her feet. Shit. One of them is bare, the other...that can't be more than a glorified slipper.

"Joey, let me carry you, buttercup."

"I can run," she says through clenched teeth. "He'll come after us..."

Trevor tosses a glance over his shoulder. "Hard right. Now!"

We veer between two darkened houses and press our backs against the wall. The sound of an engine grows louder, and Trevor signals for us to stay low and head for the barn fifty feet away. We don't have much time if we want to stay ahead of

Faruk's men, and I haul Joey into my arms and carry her the rest of the way.

"Where the hell are you, November?" Trevor whispers over comms. "November?" A few seconds later, he turns to me with a worried frown. "Nomar's gone dark. Whatever his 'complication' was...at least he disabled the gate. You two get to the Jeep and haul ass to the Mazari Sharif safehouse. I'm headed to the backup rendezvous point."

Trevor removes the saddlebags from his horse, clips them together, and throws them over his shoulders. Joey's shaking against me, and as much as I hate this plan, I have to get her somewhere safe. Fast.

"Trev?" He meets my gaze. "I'll never be able to pay you back for this."

Striding over to us, he claps his hand on my shoulder and leans in. "Family doesn't collect debts. Family does what needs to be done. Now get her out of here. And remember...if you don't hear from us by thirteen hundred tomorrow, and I mean on the fucking dot, you and Joey get out of there. Matt and his team will take care of your transpo back to the States."

"I won't leave—"

His face hardens, and all the emotion drains from his gaze. "You will. If you don't hear from us—at all—we're dead."

Joey gasps. "Trevor—?"

"I mean it." He holds out his hand to her, and she stares at him a moment before taking it. "I won't let him capture me, and neither will Nomar. We've been in this business too long. You make sure he does what I told him, okay?"

She nods as a tear trails down her cheek. "Don't die."

Trevor laughs, though even that holds little mirth. "Do my best, doc."

Before I can say a word, he slips out the barn door and into the night.

I don't want to let Joey go, but we'll be a hell of a lot faster on two horses than one. "Can you ride?" I ask.

"Pretty sure if you asked, I could fly." She offers me a weak smile, and all I can see is how she looked on our third date when we watched *The Princess Bride*. I started calling her buttercup after that, and when I wanted to tell her I loved her, but was too afraid to say the words, "as you wish" was all that came out.

Lifting Joey into the saddle, I frown when I see how bloody her right foot is. Ripping a long strip off my tunic, I tie it quickly before adjusting the stirrups for her. "You ready?" As I swing up onto the second horse and gather the reins, I meet her gaze for a brief moment. "Joey? Buttercup, I need you to stay with me for an hour. After that, we'll be safe."

"I'm not sure I believe in safe anymore," she says quietly, and we dig our heels into the horses' flanks and set off for the city.

By THE TIME we reach the Jeep, Joey's half bent over in her saddle, and she keeps shaking her head like she can't stay awake.

It's only a little after one in the morning, but I don't know what she's been through the past ten days, and though she claimed to be fine every time I asked, I haven't believed her once.

As I reach for her to help her down, she collapses into my arms with a moan. "Joey! Talk to me, baby." I cup her cheek, a yellowing bruise still swollen under my palm.

"Do...do you have any food? I haven't eaten in...a long time." Her eyelids flutter as she tries to keep them open, and she doesn't protest when I carry her to the Jeep and buckle her in.

Digging into my pack, I pull out a protein bar. "Four hundred calories of pure, unadulterated pine tar. At least that's what it tastes like. But it'll keep you going until I can get you an actual meal."

After a wobbly smile, she tears into the bar. "Oh, God. This is awful."

At least I think that's what she says. Hard to tell with her mouth full. "You're so beautiful." The words slip out before I can stop them, and Joey flinches. "Joey...I'm so sorry. I fucked everything up. Both of our lives... If I hadn't—"

"Stop." The single word is choked with emotion, and tears glisten in her eyes. "Not here. Please?" Shoving the last bite of protein bar in her mouth, she nods at the steering wheel. "If he finds us, he'll kill you, and I'll...I'll be..." She swallows a sob and shakes her head. "Just...drive."

Nodding, I stow my gear, pay the elders in the camp another five grand so they hand over the keys, and slide in next to her. Tears glisten on her cheeks, and my heart feels like it's about to break into a million pieces.

There's so much I want to say to her. So many years of regrets and desires and frustrations. But despite how strong she was when she walked into that dark basement room, now, she looks like she's about to fall apart.

I throw the Jeep into gear and head for town. I hope once we get there, she'll talk to me. Yell at me. Anything but this.

As we turn onto the main road, I whisper, "There wasn't a single day I didn't think about you. Not one."

Joey

The drive to Mazari Sharif passes in a blur. I can't quite believe I'm safe, let alone sitting next to a man I've...loved...for more than twenty years. But the reality of what happens next presses down on me, and I'm struggling to stay calm enough to breathe.

I can tell he wants to talk, but I can't. Not yet. I'm such a hypocrite. The houses start to get closer and closer together, apartment buildings and shopping centers in the distance.

Sneaking a glance at Ford's chiseled features, a hard lump in my throat aches, and I reach for the bottle of water he put in the cup holder for me. The years made him even more handsome. A hint of gray colors his temples and is sprinkled through his sandy hair. His short stubble is peppered with silver, and the lines on his forehead...he didn't have those the last time I saw him.

More than the physical, though, it's his maturity that stands out. His consideration. The way he didn't touch me until I'd made the first move. Stopping to bind my foot, and the emotion in his voice as he tried to apologize for...everything.

It doesn't take long for him to navigate through a quiet neighborhood with squat apartment buildings and old cars parked on the street. He guides the Jeep up to a garage door, hops out, and lifts it like it weighs nothing at all. The interior lights wink on as he parks, and then we're hidden away, the garage closed, the Jeep off, and Ford holding my door open.

"We're here, buttercup."

I don't have any belongings, so I slide from the seat and let him help me to the interior door. It's secured with an electronic lock, and he enters a ten-digit code, then waits for the light to turn from red to green.

"Wait right here," he says as he pulls out his pistol. "I need to clear the place. Make sure no one's been here."

A moment of pure panic consumes me, and I grab his arm. "Please don't leave me alone," I whisper.

His eyes lock onto mine, and for a second, I think he understands. How much I want to be in his arms, but how hard it is for me to ask.

"Okay. Stay behind me the entire time. *Close* behind me."

I'm practically glued to his back as he moves from room to room, checking doors and sweeping a handheld blacklight over the knobs and other hard surfaces.

In the larger of the two bedrooms, a duffel bag rests in the center of a queen-sized bed, and the lights cast a warm glow over the multi-colored, woven blanket, the pillows, and...the box of Red Vines sitting on the nightstand.

Running my hand over the wrapper, I sigh. "When Trevor found me, I didn't want to go with him. Until he showed me that little bag."

Ford's lips tug into a small grin. "You still like them?"

"Yes." The plastic rips easily, and I pull out two of the red tubes, then hand one to him. As he takes it, he looks down at my palm, then sits next to me and takes my hand, turning it over in his and unfurling my fingers.

"What happened? Did the reins cut you?"

Dammit. The half-moon cuts are bright red and one of them is still oozing a little. Sucking air through my teeth, struggling to calm my racing heart, I try to pull my hand away. "It wasn't... the reins. It doesn't...make any sense. I know it's stupid. I... I can't...explain."

"Joey, look at me."

He knows. I expect judgement, but when I meet his gaze, there's only understanding and pain. "You were trying to survive."

Only able to manage a single nod, I tense as the first tear rolls down my cheek. I can't let him see my thighs. Or my forearms. The hundreds of thin scars I've given myself over the years are so ugly, I refuse to wear shorts or tank tops, even on the hottest days of the year.

"You are beautiful, buttercup. Beautiful and strong and... we're going to talk about this. When you're ready. But for now...

these need to be cleaned—along with your foot—and then... you should rest. Will you let me help you?"

He stands, keeping my hand held tightly in his. I look up at him, the rugged, handsome man who risked his life to save me, and I wish I could tell him everything.

"Trust me, Joey. Please."

Rising on unsteady legs, I let him wrap his arm around my waist, and I lean against him. "As you wish."

12

Ford

SHE'S like a frightened little bird, shaking with every touch. Yet, there's a strength about her I can't ignore. Seated on the counter, she lets me clean the rocks and dirt from her foot, clenching her teeth at the pain.

"Ready?" I ask as I hold up the bottle of cheap vodka. The safe house's first aid kit is sorely lacking disinfectant.

"Do it." Her whimper shoots straight to my heart, but she doesn't cry, just grips the edge of the counter until her knuckles turn white.

At least there's ointment and plenty of gauze. When her foot's wrapped and I've cleaned and bandaged her palm, I carry her back to the bed. "What do you need? Food? More water?"

"To sleep somewhere no one will hurt me," she whispers, almost too softly to hear.

"You're safe here, Joey. I'll be right outside—"

"No." Grabbing my hand, she twines our fingers. "I haven't slept more than half an hour at a time since he took me." Tears tumble from her bloodshot eyes, and she sucks in a shuddering breath. "I'm afraid, Ford. If I go to sleep, will I wake up still trapped in that basement...or worse...in that train car twenty years ago? There's no way you should be here. Not after...how I left you. What I did. What happened. How do I know this is...real?"

My knees hit the ground, the truth in her voice stripping me down to my core. Framing her face, I brush my thumbs over her cheeks, skimming the tears away. The headscarf is half-askew, and I find the folds and pins holding it in place and gently loosen them, letting the dark brown material fall away from her golden locks.

"In all my dreams, I see you, Joey. What you looked like when I proposed. Your smile when I showed up on Halloween with a whole carton of Red Vines. Your eyes the day you found me in that bar." Staring down at my hands holding hers, I wish I could go back and fix what I destroyed. But I can't, so instead, I bring her uninjured palm to my lips for a gentle kiss. "Never have you felt so...*real* to me. I promise. This isn't a dream." I guide her hand to my face, to one of the bruises Faruk gave me, and offer her a weak smile. "Plus, I hope if you were dreaming of me, you wouldn't dream of an old man who just got the shit beat out of him."

Her fingers tremble as she traces the line of my jaw. And then her arms are around me, her face buried in my neck, sobs wracking her body. Her warm breath tickles my ear. Easing up onto the bed, I shift her against me, lying back so she's half draped over my chest.

We stay like that for long minutes, until her whimpers fade into rhythmic breaths against my skin. "I'm going to set a couple of extra security measures, buttercup," I whisper. But I'll be right back."

Her lashes flutter against her pale cheeks as I shift her off of me, then draw the blanket up to her shoulders. Leaving the bedroom door open so I can hear her if she wakes, I rummage through my rucksack for a roll of super thin, almost invisible wire, a small, plastic box with a blaring alarm, and a motion sensor.

In under ten minutes, I have the door and the only window that opens secured so we'll know if anyone tries to breach the safe house. Trevor and Nomar will raise me on the radio if they're close, and I set the receiver and my pistol on the nightstand within easy reach.

Their silence worries me, but this is protocol. If Nomar was blown, he'd stay quiet until he knew without a doubt it was safe. And Trevor...the guy's a ghost.

Joey whimpers in her sleep, and I stretch out next to her on top of the blankets, still wearing my boots, with the ceramic knife it its sheath under my pillow.

My entire body aches, the bruises from Faruk's beating making themselves known with every breath. But I don't care. With her next to me, nothing else matters.

HER CRY SHATTERS MY DREAMS, and she's up on an elbow, staring around the room wildly until her exhausted gaze lands on my face.

"Ford."

"I'm here, buttercup. Right here." The seconds tick by, each one seemingly lasting an hour, as I wait for her to make the next move. There's so much I don't know about this woman now, and I won't risk hurting her—no matter how much I want to comfort her.

"Will you...hold me?" she whispers. "Please."

Tugging at the woven blanket so it covers both of us, I shift onto my back and let her fit herself to my side, her head resting against my chest. "All night."

When she sighs and her eyes flutter closed, I let myself sink into the darkness with her.

Joey

I don't want to wake up. In my dreams, Ford found me. He's holding me, the solid beat of his heart under my cheek. And I'm warm. Lying on something soft. The scents of horses, blood, and sweat permeate the air, but under that, he smells like he used to. Like cedar and pine and a hint of spice.

What time is it? Zaman will come for me soon.

Panic shoots all the way down to my toes, and I jerk up—or try to—but solid arms band around me, and the bruises along my back protest. "Shhh, buttercup. You're safe."

I don't want to believe the sleepy voice rumbling in my ear, but then his stubble scrapes against my forehead, and firm lips press to my brow. "Breathe for me, baby. In and out. And open your eyes."

I do, his commanding tone impossible to ignore. It doesn't smell like my basement prison. Or anything but him. As the room comes into focus, I gasp. Bright, colorful curtains cover a window, light seeping around them. A thick patterned blanket is draped over us, and Ford stares down at me, a concerned look deepening the lines in his forehead.

"Oh God. This is real. *You're* real."

"One hundred percent authentic United States Marine, ma'am. Retired. At your service." He tries for a smile, but worry darkens his hazel eyes as he brushes a knuckle along my cheek. "You slept?"

"Yes. What...time is it?"

He checks his watch. "Almost nine. That was a solid six hours."

Rubbing my eyes to hide the tears that burn at the corners, I wriggle out of his embrace. I haven't slept that long at a stretch in...years. He put himself between me and the door, gun on the nightstand, his big body shielding me the entire time.

"Where are Trevor and...?"

"Nomar? I don't know. They haven't checked in yet. Until they do, we're on our own." Ford sits up and winces, wrapping an arm around his stomach.

"You're hurt. Oh, shit. I didn't even think...last night..." I'm a doctor. I should have remembered finding him hanging by his wrists in Faruk's torture chamber. How he leaned on me. The bruise under his right eye, his split lip.

Kneeling next to him on the bed, I reach for the buttons on his shirt. "Joey," he says, covering my hand with his. "I'm okay."

"Who's the doctor here?" Arching a brow, I wait, but he doesn't move. "I need to do this, Ford. I'd never forgive myself if you were seriously hurt and I didn't...do something."

"I've taken worse beatings from my boss in the boxing ring," he says with a wry smile. "Dax is kind of a badass—especially for a blind man."

"What?" Despite his protests, I loosen the first two buttons, and my fingers skim the light dusting of sandy hair on his chest. Memories—good ones—float at the edges of my mind, and I take a deep breath as I continue to part the dark material.

"I work for a security firm called Second Sight. So does Trevor." Ford sits up a little straighter as I reach the last button.

"A security firm? Oh no. Don't tell me you're..." I choke back a laugh, "a mall cop?"

His tunic is open now, revealing a solid six-pack and a round, raised lump of scar tissue below his collarbone.

"No!" He fakes offense with a soft snort. "We provide security and private investigative services. Dax is protecting a woman right now from a stalker who's escalating. Ella is tracking down a deadbeat dad who hasn't paid child support in

six months, and my last case before this was a rich busi-
nessman embezzling a small fortune from his wife's charity."

My last case before this...

"I'm...just a case?" My fingers still, wrapped around the
edges of the shirt. "Of course I am. Otherwise, you wouldn't
have known to look for me."

Ford cups my cheek, his hand warm and solid as he urges my
head up so he can hold my gaze. "You are *not* just a case. You are the
most important person in the world to me. Dax and I...we started
Second Sight together, but technically, he's still my boss. Owns a
majority stake in the company. *I* was supposed to be the one
protecting Evianna from her stalker. But when your sister called...
Dax didn't hesitate. Told me to take Trevor and go find you."

"Oh God. Gerry. She and my mom—"

"We'll call them as soon as we get to Kabul. I don't have a
secure phone connection out of the country from here. Just our
private comms channel. But I can get a message to Matt—he's
in charge of the team guarding Ivy and Mia—and have him call
them for you." Ford drops his hand, and the absence of his
touch sends a chill down my spine.

"There's so much...I don't know...I didn't ask last night." My
voice sounds strange as I struggle not to cry. "They're safe? Ivy
and Mia? Were they...?"

"We got to them before they were sold. Ivy hadn't been
touched. Just knocked around a little. Mia...wasn't so lucky, but
physically, she's okay, and she's a fighter. When Trevor killed
the bastard selling them, they both insisted on watching."
Concern swims in his hazel gaze, and I know he wants to ask.
But I'm not ready to tell him yet.

Instead, I nod and swallow hard. "It's my fault. They were
only taken because they were with me."

Ford cups the back of my neck and urges me to look at him.
"This is *not* your fault, Joey. Not at all. They don't blame you."

"They should. He...planned this. Planned to take me. Ivy and Mia...and...God. Ray. Our guards and translator." I'm actively sobbing now as the weight of the lives I've ruined—the lives I've ended—crashes down on me.

"I'm going to hold you, baby. Okay?" Ford asks.

I don't deserve his comfort. Or his...love. But though I can't answer him, he slowly wraps his arms around me and draws me against him. My hand rests over his heart, and the heat of his bare skin warms my palm. I've longed for this for twenty years. The man I was going to marry, the man I loved more than anything, with his arms around me, telling me everything was going to be okay.

Except, nothing will ever be okay again, and soon, he'll realize that.

When I don't have any more tears to cry, I sniffle loudly and swipe at my cheeks. *Enough. Pull yourself together. Ford's hurt. You're a doctor. Examine your patient.*

"Let go," I whisper, my voice horse. "I need to...do something. Be...useful."

Ford starts to protest, but I silence him with a pleading gaze, and he nods.

Peeling the shirt from his broad shoulders, I let my palms skim down his arms. He winces as he moves—though he tries to hide it. "Where does it hurt?"

"Left side and back." His voice is so quiet, it's almost reverent, and I lift his arm carefully. "Took some hard punches, but nothing's broken."

"I'll be the judge of that." The deep bruises are several shades of purple and blue, spreading out over his obliques before disappearing under the waistband of his pants. Tugging gently on the thin material, I expose a bit of his hip, then palpate the edges of the discoloration.

"No internal bleeding I can see," I murmur, continuing my

exploration of his body. All the way to his abs, then up to that circular scar. "What's this from?"

"Got shot year before last. Another stalking case. The guy thought I was the client's boyfriend." He shrugs, which elicits another wince, and he rolls his shoulders.

His skin is so warm, and the scent of him...familiar and not. All of this...it's the same. But so very different.

"Is this tender?" I ask as I press my fingers against his shoulder socket.

His eyes crinkle, and he clears his throat. "Yeah. Body this size isn't meant to hang from the wrists."

"Minor subluxation. No more of that, okay? No more sacrificing yourself for me or getting captured or beaten up or..." If I keep listing all the ways he could get hurt, I'll lose it completely, so I shake my head as I swallow hard. "You always were stubborn."

"I knew what I wanted. Still do."

When Ford wraps his arms around me again, I melt against his bare chest, wondering how in the world I'll survive when I lose him for the second time. Because once he knows everything? He'll realize the woman he's been pining for disappeared the minute *Jefe* and his gang of traffickers took me twenty years ago.

Ford

Having Joey in my arms...it's heaven. But a tiny moan escapes her lips as she draws back, and she pinches the bridge of her nose.

"What's wrong?"

"A little dizzy," she says softly.

Shit. "You haven't eaten. The kitchen should be fully

stocked. Let me see what I can throw together. Lie down. Rest."
I grab my gun from the nightstand and slide the holster over
my waistband.

"Ford." Her fingers are cool as they wrap around my wrist,
and the strength of her grip surprises me. "Don't leave—"

The kitchen's all of thirty feet away, but if she doesn't want
to be alone, she won't be alone. "Come on, then. Let's see if we
have the ingredients for eggs-in-a-basket."

Helping her up, I keep my arm around her waist as we
shuffle into the main room. Her limp isn't as pronounced as it
was last night, but she still leans heavily on me, and with every
step, she tenses.

In the center of the space, she stops, her gaze taking in
everything. The single window with the curtains drawn tight,
the wire stretched across the door, the black box hanging from
the knob.

"You're sure we're...safe here?"

When she tips her head up to look at me, I brush a lock of
hair behind her ear. "This place is owned by the CIA. One of
Matt's guys is monitoring the exterior cameras. The alarm will
go off if anyone tries to open the door, and there's a motion
sensor on the window there. If there's a threat coming, we'll
know."

Her body goes rigid. "Are there...cameras inside?"

"No. Why?"

With a shudder, she turns her face into my chest. "Faruk
had cameras...everywhere. The men who took us...they
watched us. After they took Ivy and Mia away, they kept me
locked in that dirty basement for at least another two days. The
toilet was just out in the open, and I could see the light from
the camera the whole time."

"Do you remember the day we met?" I have to distract her.
It's either that or I'll demand to know everything that
happened, and she's not ready for that yet.

With a choked sound that might be a sob or might be a laugh, she nods. "Bet you never thought you'd be in a wet t-shirt contest that day, did you? Or that it'd be soda. And you'd be the only contestant."

"Every soda I've had since reminded me of you." We're almost to the kitchen now, and her shoulders are no longer hiked up around her ears. "Sit down and relax, buttercup. Can I get you a blanket?" I ask as I gesture to the overstuffed brown couch.

"N-no. I'm okay."

She's not, but satisfied that she's at least not cold, I head into the kitchen and check the fridge. Perfect. I owe Trevor's contact big time. "You still do *like* eggs-in-a-basket, don't you?"

"I..." Her cheeks catch fire, and she fights a smile. "I stopped ordering them years ago. No one could ever make them like you used to."

Pride wells in my chest, followed by a brief stab of regret. It used to be Joey's favorite meal. Every time we spent the night together, I'd make it for her. "Do you want one egg or two?"

"One." Her voice lowers almost to a whisper, but I don't miss the longing in her tone. "I haven't had a full meal since they took us. If I eat too much, I'll be sick."

I go to work, starting a pot of coffee, cutting holes in pieces of bread, turning on the stove, and adding a generous pat of butter, salt, and a pinch of paprika to the griddle pan. "When Trevor and Nomar get here, we'll head to Kabul and then figure out how we're getting back to the States."

"They...he...took my passport." Joey twists the hem of her tunic in nervous fingers as I crack the eggs into their respective baskets. "Customs won't let me in..."

"We won't be going through Customs." Running a hand through my hair, I meet her gaze. "There's a lot you don't know about me, Joey. So much that's...changed. Dax and I...when we started Second Sight, we agreed on one very important thing."

Pausing to give my next words the weight they deserve, I brace my hands on the counter. "Breaking the law is acceptable—if it saves someone's life."

Questions swirl in her eyes, their blue depths paling, along with her cheeks. "Do you mean...killing people?"

"Not unless they're about to kill us. But the auctioneer? His guards? They're dead. Nomar and Trevor...they did most of the killing. But my hands aren't clean either. Not by a longshot." We're getting dangerously close to the one subject I'm terrified to discuss: our breakup twenty years ago. Flipping the toast over, I let the eggs sizzle for a brief moment, then slide them onto plates.

"You were in Iraq," she says softly as I set the dish in front of her on the coffee table, then return to the kitchen for coffee. "I know what happens in war, Ford. And why you wouldn't talk to me that night."

The empty mug in my hand crashes to the floor, shattering into a dozen pieces. Joey springs up, sways for a minute, then limps into the kitchen and drops to her knees at the edge of the destruction as I stand there, mouth dry, trying to find the words to tell her everything I couldn't all those years ago.

"Don't move." She gathers the shards, dumps them in the trash, and then steps close enough to reach up and touch my cheek. "I never blamed you."

Her eyes shimmer, her lower lip wobbling as her hand slides to the back of my neck.

"Don't say that. If I hadn't been such an ass—"

My protest dies as she ghosts her lips over mine. It's the briefest of touches, so light I fear I imagined it. Until she pulls away, her cheeks blazing. "I'm sorry. I just..."

"You never need to apologize for that, buttercup." Tangling my fingers in her hair, I dip my head, pausing just a breath away to let her set the tone, but this time when our lips meet, there's no mistaking the taste of her, or how much I want her to know...everything.

Joey wipes away a tear as she turns away and heads for the couch, and fuck. I want to haul her into my arms and confess all my sins. But I'm too much of a coward, so I snag a second mug, then sink down a foot away from her on the cushions.

Balancing the plate on her knees, she looks like she's about to cry again, and desperate for a distraction, I pick up my fork. "I have a secret ingredient. Want to know what it is?"

"If I find out," she says as she cuts into the egg and toast, "there's no reason for you to make this for me ever again." The sadness in her voice opens a thousand cracks in my heart. Her eyelids flutter as she takes her first bite, and a tiny moan escapes her curved lips.

"*That's* the only reason I need. Right there."

"What?" The word is muffled through her second forkful, but she blinks up at me, the little furrow between her brows deepening.

"That look on your face. I'd do anything to see that every day."

Sitting next to her, watching the pure joy spread across her delicate features...it's like every dream I've ever had. Except for the fading bruises on her cheek and the dark circles under her eyes.

She swallows hard and sets her fork down. "Don't, Ford."

"Don't what?" There isn't one single thing I wouldn't do to erase the sorrow in her eyes, but everything I say...it's all wrong.

"Don't make me want what I can never have. Once I get home, this—" she gestures to the plate then to me, "—will turn into nothing but a memory."

She really thinks I'll leave her. "It doesn't have to. Where's home?"

"Just outside of Boston. A little town called Quincy."

I stop with a piece of toast halfway to my mouth. "You're joking."

"Why would I joke about something like that? I've worked at St. Jude's Research Hospital for the past five years. They let me take a sabbatical to work with Doctors Without Borders." Lifting the mug of coffee to her lips, she takes a tentative sip, and the jolt of caffeine lifts a little of the dark shroud hanging over us. "Oh, I've missed this. The only coffee we could make in the camp—before—was instant. It was like flavored water."

"I live in Boston." The admission slips out before I can stop it, and Joey sputters, coffee dribbling down her chin as she frantically grabs for her napkin. "Second Sight is in the South End. I have an apartment in Charleston."

"We...we could have run into one another on the T."

I brush my fingers over hers. "If I'd known...I would have found you years ago. Joey...we could have—"

She pushes her plate away, a look on her face I can't read. Her fingers curl over her tunic, right below her neck, and she scoots back a few inches. "When...Faruk told me why he'd taken me...that he wanted me to cure his son...I knew. I *knew* I'd die there." Her voice cracks, and she holds up her hand when I try to reach for her. "He wanted me to create this drug cocktail I'd written a paper about when I was in my final year of residency. I theorized that a specific course of treatment might be able to cure the disease his son has—thalassemia. It's a blood disorder."

Wobbling to her feet, she limps over to the window and opens the drapes a crack, as if she's desperate to see the sun.

"I told him I couldn't. That his son needed a bone marrow transplant." Her fingers flutter over the bruise on her cheek. "That was the first time he hit me."

"Joey—"

She shakes her head. "Please, let me finish." I press my lips together, waiting, and she sighs. "We spent at least eighteen hours trapped in a van. Dawn until dark the first day, then...a few days after they took Ivy and Mia away, there was another full day. I couldn't see where we were going. Couldn't speak or even move."

A full body shudder shakes her thin frame, and she presses her fist against her heart. "When we crossed the border into Afghanistan, they forced me into this...metal box. It was barely big enough to lie down in, and I couldn't breathe. I passed out, thank God. I think it would have broken me."

I can't sit still any longer. Not while every word screams pain. Unsure if she'll let me hold her or comfort her, I lean against the opposite side of the window, offering her anything I can—all that I am—as she hugs herself tightly.

"Faruk planned everything. These clothes?" Joey tugs at the bottom of her tunic. "They're *my size*. The slippers? Fit perfectly. He stole me away in the middle of the night, along with Ivy and Mia—just because they were young and pretty and in the wrong place at the wrong time—killed the rest of my team, and told me one of two things would happen. Either I'd cure his son and I'd have some semblance of a life—inside the compound walls, or I'd fail, and he'd kill me."

Her fear bleeds through every word, every movement. She clenches her bandaged hand, trying desperately to dig her nails into her skin through the gauze. But as I take a step closer, she forces her fingers to uncurl.

"All I wanted," she whispers, "when I was alone at night—in that basement or in the little room Faruk locked me in—was to see you again. Just once. To get a chance to tell you..." Her watery gaze meets mine, and my heart shatters. "You were the best part of my life. And I threw it all away."

Before I can reach her, she turns on her heel and limps off into the bedroom. The bathroom door shuts with a bang, and I start after her, until the radio clicks on, and Trevor's voice booms through the air.

"Tango to Foxtrot. I'm five minutes out. Don't shoot me."

Shit.

I can't go after her. Not when Trev's almost here. But as soon as I confirm he wasn't followed and we're still safe, I have to tell her how I feel. All of it. Whatever happens afterwards, she deserves to know.

13

Ford

THE ALARM BEEPS as Trevor pulls a scooter into the small garage, and I disable the tripwire and unlock the door. He's favoring his left leg a bit as he limps up the two steps into the flat.

"What the hell happened?" I ask as I secure the door behind him.

"I couldn't find him." Trevor shuffles over to the couch, picks up Joey's half-eaten plate of eggs and toast, and raises a brow.

"Yeah. Go ahead. I'll make her another when she's hungry." That is if she ever lets me cook for her again after running away from me. And fuck me. I'm doing the same damn thing I did twenty years ago. Ignoring this *thing* between us because I'm too scared to talk to her.

Returning my focus to Trevor, I shake my head. "What do you mean you 'couldn't find him'? You went to the backup rendezvous point?"

"No, I went to Disneyland." He shoots me a look like I'm the dumbest shit on the planet, then shoves a huge bite of eggy toast into his mouth. I don't even think he chewed the damn thing. "Faruk's men showed up after a couple of hours. I killed two of them, got the shit beat out of me, and took off. I managed to get Nomar on comms for about thirty seconds, and he said he was on the move. Gave the codeword, so at least at 4:00 a.m., he was safe."

"So what do we do now?" With a frown, I check my watch. We're supposed to be out of here in a couple of hours, and I'm not ready for this private time with Joey to end. Once we're back on the transport plane...I'm terrified I'll lose her all over again.

Glancing toward the closed bedroom door, I run a hand over the back of my neck. "Listen, Joey's spooked, and I need to go talk to her. She's going to want to know what's going on."

Trevor rubs the back of his neck. "We're staying here for another twenty-four hours. If Nomar doesn't show by then... we'll go back to Kabul and take the first plane out of here."

Joey

Cracking the door, I listen to the sounds of the two men in the living room. I can't make out the words, though. I want to go out there. Find out why only Trevor came back. If Nomar didn't make it, that's one more death that's my fault.

I don't know how to do this. How to live with what I've done. All the terrible things that happened because of me. Because of my choices. If I'd never left Ford's apartment that morning... If I'd suggested a different bar for the bachelorette party... If I'd taken any of Ford's calls, read any of his letters...

A sob sticks in my throat, and I close the bathroom door, then lean against the sink and stare at myself in the mirror. I don't recognize the woman looking back at me. Too thin. Too tired. Gently, I probe my swollen cheek. The dark purple bruises are starting to fade, bits of yellow seeping in around the edges.

The sound of the slap echoes in my memories. It was louder than I expected. And then...quieter as the stars obscured my vision and I fell. Duller. And the pain went on... forever. My eyes burn, and I turn my back on the broken, hollow woman in front of me.

A stack of towels rests under the sink, and I use one to cover the mirror as I turn on the shower. I hope Ford's right and there are no cameras here. But...I can't help my paranoia. I just want to be safe.

Piece by piece, I strip and shove the clothes in the trash. Maybe Ford can find a way to burn them. The headscarf too. Stepping into the spray, I sigh. The water feels like heaven, but as I sink my hands into my hair to wash away the grime, the bruises all along my back flare, and I suck in a sharp breath, choke on the water running down my face, and double over coughing.

The position—hands on my knees—makes me want to throw up. All I can see are the dozens of tiny scars curving outward from my inner thighs. Years of cutting myself to try to feel...something...anything...and even though I'd stopped —before Faruk's men stole me away—the scars will never fade.

Panic tightens my chest, a hard ball of ice squeezing my heart. My raw throat protests the air I force through it, and I sink down onto my ass, wrapping my arms around my legs, and let the water wash away my tears. I'll never be normal. Never be able to love him. To let him love me. We live in the same city. How can I even go back there knowing I could run into him anytime?

The water starts to cool, and I push myself up, rush through washing my hair and body, and step out onto the mat, shivering, as I wrap myself in a towel.

"Joey?" Ford knocks on the door, and I clap my hand over my mouth to stifle my yelp. "Are you okay, buttercup?"

Buttercup.

He's treating me like...we're together again. Like no time has passed. Like...I'm still whole. Except, I'm not, and I never will be again. Sinking down with my back to the tub, I rest my forehead on my knees. "I need...to be alone, Ford." He'll hear the tears in my voice. He always could.

"Please, talk to me."

"There's...nothing...to say." My stupidity did this. My pride. My fear. If I'd just let him keep his secrets. Or if I'd been willing to share mine. If I hadn't managed to convince myself—despite my sister and mother's assurances to the contrary—that the reason Ford didn't contact me for a month was because he didn't want a woman who'd been broken. Who'd been used and violated in the worst ways.

I tug on the chain around my neck, palming the engagement ring he gave me so many years ago. Just a simple band, studded with tiny diamonds and sapphires. Three of each.

The FBI agent with the kind eyes and shaggy black hair knocks as he peeks into my hospital room. "Miss Taylor? Do you mind if I come in?"

I hear him, but when I try to answer, I can't force the words out. My sister takes my hand and gives it a gentle squeeze. "Joey, honey? It's Agent Beckham. You remember him."

Of course I do. I remember everything. But I don't want to.

Agent Beckham approaches the bed slowly. His was the first face I saw after they killed Jefe. He wrapped me in a blanket—one of those weird insulating ones that almost crinkle—and carried me out of that railcar. God. Was that only yesterday?

"Miss Taylor, we finished processing the warehouse next to..." He shakes his head. "The warehouse the traffickers operated out of. Most

of everyone's personal effects were gone. But we recovered a few things."

I draw in a sharp breath as he holds out his hand. My engagement ring. Sparkling clean. Ford. I wish he were here. I need him. But...I'm so...broken. Will he even want me? Tears cascade down my cheeks, and I stare at my broken finger. I can't wear it. Not now. And I want to. So much.

"Thank you, Agent Beckham," Gerry says as she takes the ring from him. "Joey's...tired. But I know she's happy to have this back."

The agent quickly darts back out of the room, and the door closes with a quiet click.

"Joey? Honey? Look at me." Gerry reaches behind her neck and unclasps her necklace. It's a simple silver chain with a pearl pendant on it—something she got for her college graduation, I think. As I blink up at her, trying to will my body to stop crying, she removes the pendant and threads the chain through the ring. "Here you go. You'll feel better having this on."

As she secures the chain around my neck, I reach for the ring. And for a moment, all the pain, all the fear, all the terrible memories fade away, and I can pretend I'm not broken.

The memory leaves me gasping for air and gripping the ring so tightly, I'm afraid I'm going to crush it.

Heavy footsteps recede, and I blow out a breath. Until, a minute or two later, they're back, and an envelope slides under the door.

"Oh, my God." His bold handwriting slashes across the front with my shaky *Return to sender* scrawled over my name.

His letters. He wrote so many. A dozen, at least. And I returned each and every one of them. I was so stupid. He kept them. He *brought* them.

My eyes burn as I rip open the flap.

I started this at least ten times. Dear Joey, Dearest Joey, My love, My Joey, My angel, Buttercup... But none of them felt right, despite every single one of them being true.

There's nothing I can say to take away your pain. There aren't any words to make what happened to you okay. And even though I was doing my job, there's no excuse for me not being there for you.

If I'd known...if I'd gotten Gerry's message the day it arrived, I'd have been on the next plane. When I came back from Baghdad, I didn't even pack. Told my CO I needed a lift to the States. Any state. I didn't care. Just somewhere that would let me get to you.

I screwed up, Joey. And I'll never forgive myself. But don't you ever say you're sorry again. You didn't ask for any of this. All you asked was for my trust. And I failed you.

I love you, buttercup. Always and forever. You're my only. My everything. And there is nothing that will ever change that. Please call me. Write me a letter. Tell me we still have a chance. I'm staying in San Diego for the next two months. Gerry says she doesn't know where you are—that you won't tell her or your mom. But if you call me, I'll be on the next plane, bus, train...whatever I need to take to get to you.

Yours...forever...

Ford

The letter falls to the floor, and my sobs echo off the tile. A second envelope lands at my feet. Then a third. A fourth. All of them. Every single message he sent me. Every single message I didn't open. Couldn't open.

I read them all, and by the time I'm done with the thirteenth—his last one, the one where he told me he'd always be there for me, always come for me—I don't think I can breathe for another minute without him. "Ford...?"

The door opens, and I look up at him, tears dripping onto the towel wrapped around me. "I'm so sorry," I manage, and his brows furrow.

"Don't ever apologize, buttercup. You did nothing wrong. Nothing at all." He drops to one knee, close enough for me to feel his warmth, yet he doesn't touch me. "We...weren't meant to be then. But we have a second chance now. If—" Ford's voice fades, and his eyes glisten as he focuses somewhere just below my neck. "Your ring..."

Wrapping my fingers around the band, I let its familiar ridges and warmth calm my racing heart. "I thought...I'd lost it forever. The man who took me...back in San Diego...he broke my finger taking it off. But when I was in the hospital, the FBI brought it back. I guess...he liked to keep...souvenirs." Swallowing another sob, I meet Ford's gaze. "I haven't taken it off in twenty years."

"Joey—"

Lurching up, I wrap my arms around him, then press my lips to his. He tastes of coffee, and he slides his arm under my knees, lifting me into his lap as he settles onto the floor.

His tongue lightly dances with mine, and I moan into the kiss. I have to do this. I have to tell him all the things I should have said twenty years ago. The secrets I've never told anyone outside the therapist who treated me when I...went away.

Ford tangles his fingers in my damp hair, and his other hand rests on my bare calf. I draw back, wishing with all my heart that I could have this conversation with him wearing more than just a towel. Except this is who I am, and I have to know if there's even the slightest chance.

His eyes...I could lose myself in his eyes. With a hard swallow, I reach up and cup his stubbly cheek. "I love you, Ford. I never *stopped* loving you. But I'm scared..." My voice drops to a whisper. "I'm too broken."

The lines around his mouth deepen, and sorrow wells in his eyes, the light hazel turning tawny. "Joey, you're perfect. You always have been. You're *not* broken."

"I am. You don't know—"

"Then tell me." Ford skims his palm up my arm, then curses under his breath. "You're cold."

Gently, he eases me off his lap, rises, and offers me his hand. As soon as I wobble to my feet, he scoops me into his arms again and carries me to the bed. When I'm safely hidden by the sheet and blanket, he takes off his boots, sets his gun on the nightstand, and slides under the covers with me.

"I should have been there for you, Joey," he says as he takes my hand and his thumb strokes back and forth over my ring finger. "I wanted to be."

A single tear trails down my cheek. "I know. And I didn't give you a chance. I didn't think you'd want to be with me. Not after..."

"Why wouldn't I want to be with you?" Hurt creeps into his voice, and he squeezes his eyes shut for a moment. The pain etched on his face is more than I can bear, and my tears spill over as he frames my face with his rough hands. "You were... raped, Joey. You didn't do anything wrong."

"I did," I whisper. "I didn't trust you. After I pushed so hard for you to trust *me*."

Ford blanches, his mouth opening and closing as he struggles for his next words. "*That's* why you wouldn't talk to me? Why you wouldn't take my calls or read my letters? I thought you'd just gotten it into your head that I'd abandoned you. God knows I gave you enough cause."

"Maybe. At first. But then Gerry said she'd called everyone she could find in the Marine Corps." I almost laugh, and the corners of my lips curve slightly. "I think she might have gotten all the way up to a Colonel at some point. And she told me you were deployed on some mission where they couldn't contact you. Since we weren't married...and I wasn't dead..."

With every word, he looks more horrified, and I lower my gaze to my hands. How much can I tell him before he runs away? Or can't stand to look at me?

"I..." Shame heats my cheeks, so hot, they feel like they're about to combust, and I can't force the words past the lump in my throat. So I do the only thing I can. I show him.

Clutching the towel to my chest, I shove the blankets down,

exposing my legs. He's still staring at my face, so I guide his fingers over my thigh. Over the dozens of scars that mark me as...damaged. As too weak to deal with my own emotions. And too scared to trust anyone else with them.

"Did he do this to you? The piece of garbage who took you?"

If only that were true. "No. I did it to myself."

Ford

I didn't see it. The cuts on her palm. The scratches on her arms. Hell, I had her half-naked in my lap just a few minutes ago. I have so many questions, but the only one that escapes is, "Why?"

"Everything hurt," she whispers. "Every noise terrified me. We'd fall asleep...and they liked to wake us up by—" With a shake of her head, she says more than she could with any words. "When the FBI came, *Jefe*—that's what he made us call him—put a gun to my head. He was going to kill me. So I punched him in the balls."

She's so matter-of-fact. Almost like she's watching someone *else's* memories. How the FBI shot the asswipe. How he landed on top of her. The hospital. The humiliation of being examined, of being forced to tell her story over and over again. "The mind can only take so much pain," she says, her voice hoarse. "When I felt like I was disappearing, when I couldn't feel *anything*, doing...this...let me breathe again."

"This is what you couldn't tell me?"

She doesn't speak. Just nods.

My frustration edges towards anger. But not with Joey. With myself. Forcing out a breath, I gently turn her arm so I can see the scars running from her elbow all the way down to her wrist.

Most are old, but there are two fresh ones. Tracing one, I steal glances at her face, watching for any reaction. There's nothing in the pale, blue depths of her eyes. Shell-shock. Or something close to it. So many of the guys I served with...they wore that same look.

So I do the only thing I can. Gather her close, bring her wrist to my lips, and kiss each mark on her skin. By the time I reach the last one, she's back with me—her free hand clutching my shirt.

"You're beautiful, Joey. Beautiful and brilliant and perfect and the best thing to ever happen to me. There is nothing you could ever do that would make me stop loving you. I only have one question."

Her breath hitches, and she bites her lower lip so hard, it turns white. "What?"

"Do you...*will you* trust me now?"

I see her struggle. Her shame. But more than that...I see hope. A hint of that light in her eyes I feared she'd never find again.

Her fingers brush my cheek, and her answer rights my entire world.

"Yes."

14

Ford

I DIDN'T WANT to leave her. Not even for a minute, but these clothes have seen better days, and the scent of blood—mine and hers—doesn't take either of us happy places. So now, under the shower spray, I clench my fists at my sides, letting the hot water ease some of the knots in my shoulders and back.

Holding her felt so right, so familiar, despite how much we've both changed. And when she relaxed against me, burying her face against my neck, it was like coming home.

Not wanting to be away from her for long, I rush through the shower, ignoring the stubble covering my cheeks. My shoulder still throbs, but having Joey with me, truly *with* me, eases the rest of the discomfort from Faruk's *interrogation*.

With a towel around my waist, I pause with my hand on the door knob. She trusts me. She's seen me naked a hundred times. But this is all new. We're two strangers in love, and I don't know where the lines are.

Time to find out.

When I throw open the door, Joey's back is to me, but she

whirls around, her panicked gaze scanning the room. Words of reassurance die in my throat as I register the bruises covering her back around her bra straps and peeking out of the waistband of her black pants.

You're a fucking idiot. You saw that asshole kicking the shit out of her and you never even asked.

"God, Joey. You're hurt." I take two steps closer to her, and she tenses, but then gives me a little shake of her head.

"I'm okay. Nothing's broken."

This close, she has to crane her neck to meet my gaze, and I hold out my hand until her delicate fingers touch my palm, then sink down onto the bed with her still standing in front of me. "Will you let me see?" I don't take my eyes off hers as I bring the back of her hand to my lips. After a moment, I add, "Trust takes time, buttercup. I won't force you."

As if I've just said the magic words, she takes a deep breath, and her shoulders relax as she turns around.

"Can I touch you?"

Flexing her hand several times, she stutters, "Y-yes." When my fingers brush along the border of one of the worst of the bruises, she flinches and makes a fist hard enough I can see the blood leave her fingers. Just as I'm about to tell her to stop, though, she relaxes, her hand uncurls, and I think I hear her whisper, "Let yourself feel."

"What?" I'm frozen in place—one hand on her back, the other curved around her hip. "Talk to me, baby."

Her head bows, and she lays her hand over mine. "Before this trip, I hadn't hurt myself in years. But for a long time, I couldn't stop. I was numb. Like...I moved through life rather than experiencing it. Because if I let myself feel—anything—I'd feel everything. Their h-hands on m-me. The dirty f-floor."

As a sob shakes her entire body, I take a chance and wrap my other arm around her, pulling her between my legs and against my chest.

The contact seems to steady her, and she clears her throat. "Cutting let me feel something *I* controlled. The pain helped me focus. And...before long, I *needed* it. The only time I felt *anything* was when I cut myself. But then I found a new therapist, and she helped me understand that not every one of my feelings would hurt me. Some of them...could help me heal."

Twisting in my embrace, she faces me, her eyes clear, and offers me the barest hint of a smile. "I used to love it when you'd touch me. Just...touch. You'd rub my back in bed when you thought I was asleep. And after...we made love...you'd run your fingers up and down my arm."

Her left arm holds deep finger bruises, but I start stroking her right bicep, the smooth muscle relaxed and supple under my hand. "I couldn't get enough of you, Joey. I still can't..." It doesn't matter that we're not there yet, or that Trevor's in the next room. Not to my dick. Half-hard and getting more insistent by the minute, the damn thing starts tenting the towel, and when Joey notices, she sucks in a sharp breath.

"Ford, I don't know how much I can give you..." Sorrow creeps into her tone, and her shoulders hunch.

"I don't care."

Snapping her gaze to mine, she shakes her head. "Ford—"

"Baby, you're it for me. You always have been and you always will be. If this—holding you—is all we ever have, if this is all you can ever give me, I'll still be the happiest man in the world. Do I want all of you? Hell yes. And I'll give you all of me. But only if...or when...you're ready."

The storm raging in her eyes settles. "I don't deserve you," she whispers. Before I can correct her, she wraps her arms around me. "But you're it for me too." When she kisses me, something flares, bright and hot, and it isn't until she pulls away and reaches for her shirt that I put a name to the feeling.

Hope.

Joey

It feels so good to be wearing "normal" clothes. Tennis shoes. Socks. The black pants hang off of me, but the tank top alone makes me feel more human. I stare at the purple, long-sleeved blouse designed to cover me when outdoors, and for the first time in years, I wonder what it would be like not to hide my arms.

Ford knows now. Everything. Or...almost everything. I didn't technically *tell* him I haven't had sex in twenty years, but he probably figured that part out.

"You don't have to, buttercup," he says as he pulls on a black t-shirt. The material hugs his chest and leaves the corded muscles of his forearms bare. I always loved his arms. His strength.

An unfamiliar warmth stirs deep in my center, and I don't realize I'm staring until he says my name.

"Don't have to what?" I ask as I tear my gaze away from his biceps.

"Cover up." His fingers skim the lines on my skin. "Just keep it close in case we have to run."

My muscles lock, and it's almost like I can *hear* panic flooding my system as his words register. "Do you think that's—?"

His eyes soften, and he links our fingers. "No. I don't. But I'm not taking any chances with your safety." Ford cups my cheek, dips his head, and brushes a soft kiss to my lips. "I can't lose you again."

When he touches me, it's like all of my anxiety melts away. As I tie the blouse around my waist, Ford laces up his boots and slides his holster onto his belt.

"Ready?" he asks, his hand on my lower back.

In truth, I want to burrow under the blanket and hide. But I nod and let him open the door for me.

Trevor's hunched over a laptop on the couch, typing furiously, two energy drink cans at his elbow.

"Any word from Nomar?" Ford asks.

With a grunt, Trevor pushes to his feet, grabs the empty cans, and limps off towards the kitchen for another of the caffeinated drinks. "Not really. I got a single blip on the radio an hour ago. But all I heard before he cut out was the passphrase and him saying "twenty-four hours."

"You're hurt." I eye his gait as he heads back with a fresh can. "What happened?"

Focusing on me, as if he didn't realize I was even here until just now, he shakes his head. "Just my ankle. It'll heal. You okay?" His gaze lingers on my arms, but rather than focusing on the scars, he seems to be more concerned with the bruises.

With a roll of my eyes, I point to the couch. "Sit. Take your shoe and sock off. I'm a doctor, remember?"

Trevor arches a brow at Ford as he drops down. "I'd do what she says, Trev." Ford chuckles as he opens the fridge and rummages around inside. "You hungry, buttercup?"

"Yes. Very." For the first time since this whole ordeal began, I feel...comfortable. Like I could eat. Sleep. Laugh. Even though we're still trapped in Afghanistan, Faruk is probably hunting for me, and too many people have died, there's something normal about Ford offering to cook for me and examining a patient, checking for injuries.

"You sure you want to do this?" Trevor asks as he prepares to pull off his boot. "My last shower was a while ago."

"Unless you've suddenly developed gangrene, I've seen worse. Actually, scratch that. Even if you have, I've seen worse. Off." Patting my knee, I wait for him to strip off his sock and put his foot up. His entire ankle is swollen, but there's little to no bruising and as I manipulate the joint, he only winces a little.

"Just a mild sprain. I can wrap it for you. Let me get the first aid kit."

When I'm done, he flexes his toes, stands, and eases his weight onto the foot. "Damn good wrap job, Doc. Ford, I'm going to catch a few hours. The encrypted connection on the laptop's a little spotty, but you should be good to contact Dax and have Joey message her family. Just don't tell anyone where we are or when we're coming back."

"Do we even *know* when we're going home?" I ask.

"Soon," Trevor replies. "We'll give Nomar until twelve hundred tomorrow, then we're getting the fuck out of this country. If he doesn't show by then, we'll call in Ryker. You might want to give him a heads up."

With a nod to Ford, Trevor limps off to the second bedroom, shuts the door, and a few seconds later, there's a dull thud like he literally fell over onto the bed.

"I don't think he's slept in thirty-six hours," Ford says. As I join him in the kitchen to wash my hands, my stomach rumbles. He's already diced fresh fruit and portioned it out into bowls, and buttered bread for grilled cheese sandwiches.

"We can really get in touch with my family?" I ask. "It's safe?"

Ford wraps his arm around my waist and buries his face in my hair. "Email only, but yes. It's safe. Wren—she works with us at Second Sight—is a tech genius. No one goes into the field without her equipment."

"There's so much I don't know about you." Resting my cheek against his chest, I listen to his heartbeat, the strong, steady thumping easily my new favorite sound. I fell asleep to it last night—or this morning. Whenever he held me. And now... it's like my touchstone. This is real. He's real. And he's mine. My throat tightens, emotion threatening to steal my words, but I tip my head up to meet his gaze. "Tell me about Second Sight."

15

Joey

OUTSIDE THE WINDOWS, darkness shrouds the quiet neighborhood. I spent the afternoon in Ford's arms. Curled on the couch talking about...everything and nothing. His job. His coworkers and friends: Dax, Wren, Clive, and Ella. How much he loves helping people. My time with St. Jude's. The kids I've helped save. The ones I've lost.

Trevor emerges from the second bedroom, and I jerk at the sound, but it only takes me a few seconds to relax now. It's amazing how reassuring it is having two lethal men with guns on my side for a change. "I slept all day," he says as he sinks onto the sofa and grabs his laptop. "I'll keep watch tonight. You two can get some shuteye."

Apparently I look as tired as I feel. Despite the rest I found in Ford's arms when we arrived, I haven't had more than an hour at a time since I was taken, and though it's only a little after 8:00 p.m., I'm exhausted. Also...nervous. We talked so much, even kissed a little. But what happens now?

Ford links our fingers and helps me to my feet. The look he

gives me...his hazel eyes are so intense, my insides clench—a subtle warmth creeping all the way down to my toes, and I *want* more. More than I've ever wanted since we were last together.

Staring at the bed as he shuts the door, I fumble for the shirt still tied around my waist. "Do we...need to be ready to run?" I ask.

"There's been no sign—"

When his answer comes from right behind me, I yelp softly and whirl around, my hands slapping against his strong chest hard enough to send him stumbling back a step. "Oh God. I'm sorry. I..." With a shake of my head, I shrink away and focus on my breathing to get my heart rate back down to something close to normal.

"What's wrong, buttercup? What did I do?" Ford's so apologetic, so worried, but to his credit, he doesn't follow me. Just stands still and watches me with concern.

"I...I can't stand anyone coming up behind me. It's stupid. I knew you were in the room. I asked you a question. But—"

"You can't reason with PTSD, Joey." Ford sinks down onto the mattress, choosing the side closest to the door. "No coming up behind you. Noted. You don't have to explain unless you want to."

Now I feel even worse. "I do. But I don't know how. Not without...going back there. And I can't...not yet. Not here."

Nodding, he reaches for the edge of the blanket. "Can I hold you tonight?"

"I was hoping you would." My cheeks warm, and I can't figure out how to explain what I need. And what I don't. But when he takes off his boots, then shoves his legs under the covers, I stop unlacing my sneakers to stare at him. "Ford? I'm not that...delicate." His brows draw together. "When we were together before...we slept naked. Or you'd sleep in your briefs. You can't tell me you've started sleeping fully clothed in the last twenty years, just because."

Frustration stiffens his shoulders. "Joey, you're the most important person in the world to me. There's nothing I wouldn't do for you. But this is all new territory for me."

"Me too." Though I don't remove my tank, I unbutton my pants and let them fall to the floor, exposing my scarred thighs and black panties. A groan rumbles in his chest, and my nipples tighten under the bra and tank. I don't know where my sudden burst of bravery comes from, but this is Ford. The man I was going to marry. He's seen me naked. Or...at least the twenty-two-year-old version of me.

"I want you to be comfortable, baby. If you need me to sleep with my boots on every night for the rest—" he shakes his head, "I will."

For the rest of our lives. That's what he was going to say. A smile tugs at my lips, and for a moment, I feel like I'm normal. Like I'm not broken. Not damaged. Not scarred. Like maybe we'll be able to come back from everything that's happened and find our happy ever after.

"I can handle you without pants."

"Only if you're sure."

At my nod, he gets to his feet, and then he's standing across the bed from me wearing only his black briefs, and I can't look away. The bulge in the material makes me long for more, and an unfamiliar need stirs deep inside.

"I want to be close to you," I whisper. That's not all I want, but it's all I can manage to say for the moment. Snuggling up to him, I rest my hand on his chest, the light sprinkling of hair tickling my fingers. "You've changed so much. The last time we were together like this..."

"The last time, that hair under your fingers wasn't partly gray."

My laugh settles me, and I lean up on an elbow. "I like it. Makes you look distinguished."

"You mean old, right?" Ford brushes a lock of hair away

from my face and trails his knuckle along my jaw. "We wasted so much time."

"How did Gerry find you?" Getting comfortable again, I let the steady beat of his heart calm me. "Because if she knew you were in Boston all this time, she and I are going to have words."

"Don't be mad at her. She hired an old cop friend to track me down. I don't think she had any idea." He skims his hand up and down my arm, just like he used to. "I swear to God, Joey, if I'd known...I'd have been at your door every damn day until you told me to go to hell or let me in."

"I wish I could say I would have let you in. I just...don't know. I'm not...someone you should want to be with." He starts to ask me why, and I stop him with my finger to his lips. "I haven't had sex since it happened."

Ford collapses back against the pillows, staring up at the ceiling. "So the last person you were with was—"

"You." After a shuddering breath, I sit up so I can face him. "What happened to me...wasn't sex. It took me a long time to realize that. He and his men...they hurt us in so many ways. But what they did to us wasn't sex. It was violence and pain and humiliation." I pause and wait for him to look at me. "You're the only person I've ever made love to."

Ford pulls me against him, and his arms tighten around my waist. "Is this okay?"

"It's perfect." Nestling my head in the crook of his neck, I breathe him in. Even here, in a foreign country, on the run, his natural scent, the one I think he was practically born with, carries through. A hint of pine, cedar, and a light spice. And everything I want. But even though he's been amazing today, I'm still terrified for my next words. "I don't know if I can have sex ever again. I dated a few times over the years. But whenever we got to the physical part of the relationship, I'd bail. Find some excuse to give up on things and run. Eventually, I stopped even trying."

"That's why we're going to talk about what you want and don't want, buttercup. All of it. I need to know what makes you nervous. What scares you. Anything you're not 100% positive about. I want to know..." he cups my cheek and brushes his thumb over my lips, "all of it."

"Ford—"

"I won't push you, Joey. If you need a week, a month, a year...before you can talk to me about what happened, I'll wait. As long as you're with me—as long as you trust me with what you're feeling *now*—I'll wait forever if I have to."

Ford

She's so beautiful. So strong and brave. But when I came up behind her, the look in her eyes—pure terror. Now, trepidation laces her tone, but it feels so damn good to have her legs tangled with mine, her hand on my chest, her hair tickling my neck.

"I want it all, Ford. I want to be normal again. To feel like... like I used to." Wriggling up slightly, she leans in. The kiss starts out gentle, almost chaste, and then her tongue darts out and traces the seam of my lips. I yield, and pure, raw need for her shoots down to my dick. With one of her legs thrown over mine, she quickly notices my arousal, and against my chest, her heartbeat quickens.

"Slow down, buttercup," I whisper as I break off the kiss and run my hands up and down her back, trying to avoid her bruises. "We have all the time in the world. Tell me what you like."

"I...I don't know." Her hooded eyes hold fear, but also desire. "Touch me."

"One word, and I stop. Okay?" I lay her down, brushing her

hair away from her face. "If you feel anything but pleasure, you have to tell me, Joey."

"I will."

I'm not sure I believe her. She wants this so badly, I'm afraid she'll push herself too far without even realizing it. Dipping my head, I start to kiss along her jaw. "You used to like this," I say against the delicate skin behind her ear.

"Oh...yes," she says, her voice breathy as goosebumps prickle all along her arms.

"And this?" Continuing my exploration down the curve of her neck, I scrape my teeth over the sensitive tendon there, biting down gently until a little gasp escapes her lips. A burst of her scent—of her arousal—washes over me, and then she draws in a sharp breath and her entire body goes still.

"Joey? What's wrong?" Concerned I pushed her too far, I sit up and rest my hands on her shoulders. "Talk to me, buttercup."

A slow smile spreads across her lips. "I wasn't sure...I didn't think I'd ever be able to again..."

"I don't understand."

Urging me to lie back down, Joey gazes up at me, love darkening the blue of her eyes. "You will. Keep going."

I'll give her anything she wants. She's my entire world. Running my finger under the strap of her tank, I arch a brow. "May I?"

She bites her lip, but nods, and when I strip off the dark material, leaving her in just her bra, she frowns.

"What is it?"

"The bra too." The boldness in her words shocks me, but I do as she asks, reaching behind her to unsnap the hooks. Her breasts spill out of the black cotton, her nipples already hardened into tight nubs.

My dick aches, and damn. If she even touches me, I'm afraid I'll explode. I never told her—she's not the only one who hasn't had sex in fucking forever. I've fooled around, sure. Had a few girlfriends I went down on. And hand jobs in the shower? I'm a damn expert. But actual sex? I could never bring myself to that point. It felt like a betrayal.

"Ford?" The whispered word brings me back from my own momentary reverie, and I meet her gaze. "Touch me."

Cupping her breast, I take one taut nub between my lips, and she arches her back, moaning softly. "Oh God. I'd forgotten..."

"What?" I say after laving my tongue over the peak again and again, delighting in her quick pants, the way her hands fist in the sheets, and the blush breaking out over her dewy skin.

"How to *feel*..."

I pinch the other nipple, and Joey shudders, clamping her hand over her mouth to contain the constant little whimpers and gasps she makes as I kiss, suck, and nip my way lower. She smells like the sea after a storm, her arousal wrapping around me like a cloak, and when my lips brush the waistband of her panties, I stop, gazing up at her from between her legs.

"We can stop, baby. Nothing else has to happen." My hands are clamped around her hips, my cock threatening to break free from my briefs. I want her so badly. Want to bury myself deep inside her and feel her clench around me.

Our last night together before the end plays over and over in my mind.

"I like you balls-deep in me."

God. She was so...direct. Still is, when she's not scared of saying the wrong thing or doing something that will trigger bad memories. She's still my warrior. It's still inside her. Buried under all that pain.

Joey takes one of my hands and threads her fingers with mine. Slowly, she guides me under the hem of her panties and over her mound.

"Fuck, baby. You're so wet," I whisper, and then look up to

see her eyes shining and her lower lip caught between her teeth. Fear snakes its cold tendrils around my heart, and I freeze until she releases her lip and smiles.

"I didn't think I would ever want this again," she says, her voice halting and rough. "Or be able to do this. I've kissed other guys. I tried vibrators. Even watched porn. Nothing. I felt... nothing. I thought...I thought that part of me died twenty years ago. But...it hasn't. It was just...waiting for you."

Pride puffs out my chest—both for being the one to reintroduce her to herself, and for being with someone who's so brave, who can fight her way back from so much pain to let me touch her. To even let me hold her.

I watch her face carefully as I slide the panties down her hips, and fuck, the scent of her, the way her dark blond curls glisten, the shift of her hips as I position myself between her thighs...I'll be lucky if I don't lose control the second I taste her.

"We can stop—"

"Shhh. Trust me, Ford. And...make me come. Please." A tear slips down her cheek, and I reach up and flick it away.

"As you wish."

Joey

I never imagined it would be this easy. Every time I tried to fool around with a guy, it always ended in panic, tears, and shame. But with Ford...there's none of that. Only tenderness and love and a need so great, I feel like I'm about to come out of my skin.

He nuzzles my curls, inhaling deeply, his chest rumbling with an almost feral growl. And then his tongue touches my lower lips, and my world explodes into light and color. My core tightens, pleasure shooting all the way down to my toes.

"Fuck, Joey. You taste like heaven," he says against my clit, and the combination of his words and the breath whispering over my sensitive nub almost make me come right then. But he pulls back slightly so we can lock eyes. Every move, every time he ups the intensity, he checks with me, like I'm his entire world and the sex is all about me.

I want to give him every bit as much as he's given me. But I don't know how. When he finds reassurance in my gaze, he smiles, and his tongue goes back to work. All thoughts of pleasing *him* flee as he licks and kisses, sucks and even bites gently.

Lust, need, desire, and a desperate ache consume me. My hips grind against his mouth, my toes curl. "More," I gasp, the only word I can force past my lips, and he slips a finger inside me.

A split second of panic shoots through my body, but it's immediately replaced with a pleasure so intense, so overwhelming, I let go.

"Ford!" I choke out. "Yes! Oh God. Yes!"

My world dissolves into flashes of light, and the only sound is the dull roar of my heartbeat in my ears. Ford's everywhere. His kisses. His hands. His love.

And I'm flying. Floating away so high, I might never come back down.

16

Ford

THIS IS THE BEST DREAM. Joey's hair tickles my nose, her sweet scent surrounding me. Skin to skin, we're tangled together under the blankets, her arm around my waist. What's even better? She's naked. Her fingers curl against my side, and my eyes fly open. She's not the only one who can't believe we're here, apparently,

"'Morning," she whispers with a little smile.

Twisting a lock of her hair around my fingers, I press a gentle kiss to her lips. "Did you sleep?"

"All night. I haven't slept all night..." she buries her face in my neck for a moment, "since I left you twenty years ago."

The admission rips through my heart, tearing and twisting my guilt until I pull away, throw my legs over the side of the bed, and rest my elbows on my knees, head in my hands. "I should have been there. Every day. Every night."

"We can't keep having this conversation." Skimming her palm over my back, she scoots closer. "We both made mistakes. We're here now. We can move on. You said you wanted to start over. Starting over implies...letting go of the past. Or at least... not letting it consume us."

Peering up at her, I see the hope in her eyes. The blankets pulled up under her arms, hiding her body. And the tinge of embarrassment on her cheeks. "Please. Lie here with me a little longer. We have...a little longer, don't we?"

With a quick check of my watch, I nod. "We should let Trev get some sleep before noon, but it's only 6:00 a.m. He won't expect us to relieve him until eight." Taking her wrist, I gently move her arm way from where she clutches the blanket. "You don't ever need to hide from me, buttercup."

"Habit," she says as her cheeks darken in the dim light from the bedside lamp. "I don't *do* this." Gesturing to the bed, then to her body, still mostly hidden, she slides back under the blankets. "Not when I'm alone...*definitely* not with anyone else around."

"Joey, there's something I didn't tell you last night." I join her, and she tangles her legs with mine. The contact only makes my dick harder, and I groan as I try to shift her slightly.

I'm still wearing my briefs. After Joey's release, she couldn't string two words together, exhaustion and pleasure conspiring to drag her to sleep. So when she reached for me with a slurred "your turn," I pulled her against me and stroked her back until she passed out.

"What is it?" Undeterred, she skims her hand down my abs, tracing each muscle until she finds my cock. "Because I seem to remember you promising me we'd finish what we started."

For all her nervousness the previous night, now, she's almost brazen. Except, fear lingers in the depths of her gaze. She wants this, but she's still terrified. "We will. If you want to." Linking our fingers, I bring our hands to rest over my heart. "But only if you're ready. Can you tell me, without a doubt, you're ready?"

Joey bites her lower lip, and her fingers flex in mine. For a brief moment, it's like a dark cloud settles over her, but then it's gone. "Yes. I'm tired of being scared, Ford. Tired of the nightmares. Of never feeling comfortable in my own skin."

Flopping back against the pillows, she stares up at the ceiling. "Nothing you or I do will take back those twenty years. The five days I spent trapped in that railcar being...*raped*. The ten days Faruk had me. I'll never be...whole again. For the rest of my life, I'll be...damaged. But I don't have to be so damaged I can't function.

"Every one of my therapists have told me I can be broken and still be...worthy of love. Until yesterday, I didn't believe them. But now...maybe I understand. Just a little."

"Baby," I prop myself up on an elbow so she can see my face. "You are not broken. You're perfect."

The look she gives me is one part "you don't understand" and one part "you're an idiot."

"So, what did you need to tell me?" Joey cups my cheek, my stubble rasping against her thumb as she traces the line of my jaw.

"I dated now and then, Joey. Three or four women over the years. But none of them...we'd fool around. They'd get off. Sometimes they'd give me a hand job in the shower. But... something always stopped me from taking it any further."

"Wait. You...haven't had sex in twenty years?" Shock infuses her tone, and she scrambles back against the pillows, pulling the blanket to her chest again. "Ford, my God. You're...you're like...um...super hot. Women should have been throwing themselves at you. And you should have been catching them."

"I didn't want them." With a shrug, I meet her gaze. "I only ever wanted you."

Joey

When Ford kisses me, all of my worries melt away. Even here, on the run, in a tiny apartment in a country where we could be killed in some neighborhoods just for having an American accent, nothing can touch me in his arms. Rolling on top of him, I press my hips to his, feeling the hard bulge of his erection against my thigh.

Fear ripples through me. Memories of all the times I was forced—either on my knees or taken from behind—and I whimper, but as I draw in a breath, I scent him. The man I love. The man who saved me and asked me a dozen times the previous night if I was comfortable. If I was ready.

"What are your triggers?" His fingers comb through my hair, and he holds my gaze. "What shouldn't I do?"

"Just...face me. I can't...go down on you. Not...yet." *Maybe not ever.* "Just...go slow."

Reaching into the duffel bag next to the bed, Ford pulls out a strip of condoms and drops them on the pillow. "Slow it is."

He snags the waistband of his briefs and slides them down his hips, freeing his erection, and I stare at the wide, smooth shaft, the dark skin of his crown, and the bead of precum leaking from the tip.

I used to love sex with him. He filled me in a way that left me feeling...like nothing else could ever touch me, and I need that sensation again. My fingers tremble as I reach for him, and when I wrap them around his girth, he shudders. "Oh God, Joey. I won't last long."

Grabbing the foil packet, I try, unsuccessfully, to tear it open and roll the condom over his length. Ford stills my frantic efforts with his hands on mine, and when he meets my gaze, he offers me a tight smile. "Relax, buttercup. Take a deep breath. Focus on my voice. You're so beautiful. So strong. I love you."

The timbre of his words does with no anti-anxiety drug ever

could—calms me and centers me—and once he's sheathed, he asks, "Do you want to be on top?"

"N-no. I want you to make love to me."

Straddling me, he nudges my entrance with his tip, and I lock my eyes onto his. I'm prepared for pain, for panic, but all I feel is...a delicious fullness as he slides home an inch at a time. So full. So...completely his.

"Tell me if this is too much," he whispers against my lips. "Too fast, too hard, too...anything."

And in that moment, I know...there's nothing he could possibly do that I couldn't come back from. My scars are my own. Made by bad men so many years ago, it feels like another lifetime. And while I'll always remember, always be broken, with Ford, I'm who I'm supposed to be.

"Too perfect," I say as I wrap my arms around his neck. "I want to feel you come, Ford. Please. Make me...yours again."

***

Ford

As I lace up my boots, Joey plops down next to me on the bed and gives me a hard stare. "You had an entire strip of condoms in your bag. You were *that* confident you'd find me? And that I'd be willing—"

"No," I say, forceful enough it almost sounds like a growl. "Shit. I'm sorry, baby." Lowering my voice almost to whisper, I wait until Joey's eyes no longer look like saucers. "I was certain I'd find you. Because I wasn't going to leave until I did. But these...they're part of our standard go-bags."

"You regularly have sex on your protective details? Some of you?"

I chuckle, running my hand through my hair. "No, but better safe than sorry. Trev's bedded a few women over the years. Pretty sure Clive has too. Even Ella took a suspect to bed when she was a cop. Though, I think that was the case that ended her career. She rarely talks about it."

The look she gives me is skeptical at best, but then she bumps her shoulder into mine. "Well, no more condoms in your go bag, Marine. You're mine now."

"Yes, ma'am." I stand and salute her, and she laughs. Not the tight, stressed out laugh I heard once or twice yesterday, but the laugh I remember. And when I meet her gaze, the light in her eyes is enough to make me take a step back in awe. "There you are, buttercup," I whisper as I take her into my arms. "I knew I'd find you."

TREVOR GRUNTS, "ABOUT DAMN TIME," when we emerge from the bedroom a few minutes after eight. "Nomar's on his way. Got a message from him twenty minutes ago. Nothing but clock time—oh-eight-thirty—and "need medical.""

At my side, Joey tenses. "Can we get more supplies? The first aid kit's been pretty decimated. Between my foot and Trevor's ankle..."

"Not without one of us leaving. And every time we leave this building, we risk being seen by the wrong people." I rest my hand on her lower back and wait until she peers up at me. "Let's hang tight until Nomar gets here. If you can't treat him with what we have on hand, I'll go out."

Fear turns her eyes a paler blue, and she hugs herself tightly. "Don't leave me," she whispers. "Please. Not here."

As Trevor shuts the door to the second bedroom, I frame her face with my hands. "Joey, I'm never going to leave you again. But if Nomar's hurt, I can't just let him suffer. Not after he risked so much for me—for both of us. And I worry about you on the streets. Trev hasn't said anything, but we don't know if Faruk is looking for you. Or if he is...where. I trust Trevor with my life. You can too." Reluctantly, she nods, and I guide her into the kitchen. "Want to try eggs in a basket again?"

WE'VE JUST FINISHED breakfast when the radio crackles to life next to me. "Open the damn door.."

"Authentication code: Nine-Seven-Alpha-Oscar," I say.

"Foxtrot-Charlie," Nomar confirms.

Joey stares at me like I've grown a second head as I head for the door. "What was that all about?"

"If he'd responded Golf-Foxtrot-Yankee, it would have meant he was compromised. Foxtrot-Charlie means no one's following him or coercing him." Disabling the tripwire for a second time, I flip the deadbolt, detach the chain, and let him in.

"Oh, my God," Joey cries as she rushes past me. "Mateen."

In his arms, Nomar holds Faruk's son. The boy's mother clings to the NSA operative, and all three of them look like they're about to pass out. Joey touches Mateen's forehead, peers into his eyes, and then leans down to...sniff him? "Lisette? Why didn't you tell me he was diabetic?"

"He's not," Lisette protests, fear in her green eyes. "But last night, he started to complain that everything hurt."

Joey curses under her breath. "He's in ketoacidosis. His liver is malfunctioning. Mateen? Do you remember me?"

"Dr. Joey," he slurs. "Mama said..." His eyes flutter closed, and he falls silent.

"Get him onto the couch." Joey points behind her, and Nomar shuffles over with a grunt and lays the boy down.

"Trev!" I shout. "Get the fuck out here. Now."

Joey kneels next to Mateen, but as she rests her fingers on

his carotid artery, her head whips towards Nomar. "Ford...? Nomar's hurt. Check on him—basic field triage."

I take two steps towards them when Nomar staggers back, hits the small table off the kitchen, and falls onto his ass. His entire left side is covered with blood, and he's breathing heavily.

"He was shot," Lisette says quietly. "By Zaman as we were fleeing the compound. But he would not let me do anything to help him. We had to keep moving. I used my headscarf to tie around him."

Trevor bursts into the room, bleary-eyed and exhausted, but as soon as he sees Nomar on the floor and Mateen on the couch, he looks to me. "What the hell is this? We're not running an escape train here. Our mission was Joey, Ivy, and Mia."

"Shut the fuck up," I mutter as I lift Nomar's shirt and then untie the makeshift pressure bandage. "Joey, it's bad." Blood oozes from the wound, and while I don't think he's about to bleed out, there's so much already soaked into his shirt and the headscarf that the bullet has to still be inside him.

"Nomar," I say as I slap his cheek lightly. His eyes are mostly closed, and his breathing labored. "Stay with me, man. You're gonna be okay." I hope to God I'm right.

Joey tells Lisette to get Mateen a glass of water and make him drink it, then turns around to check on Nomar. She palpates around the wound and hisses out a breath. "It's infected. Trevor, I need the first aid kit. Any supplies you have. And that bottle of vodka. Nomar? I'm Joey. Tell us what happened, okay? You need to keep talking."

"I...had to," Nomar manages. "I saw them as I...was trying to escape, and Faruk was wailing on her." He shudders when Joey presses hard just above the bullet hole.

First aid kit in hand, Trevor drops down next to her, and Joey digs out a pair of tweezers. She unbuckles Nomar's belt, folds it in half, and offers it to him. "This is going to hurt, Nomar. A lot. Bite down."

He nods, and as Joey pours vodka over the wound, the leather trapped between his teeth muffles his scream.

"Good. Just one more thing, and then you can rest." After she spills some of the vodka on a pair of tweezers, she meets my gaze. "Hold his shoulders, Ford. He needs to be very, very still."

I press down on his shoulders and Trev grabs his legs. As Joey digs into the wound, Nomar's entire body stiffens, his back arches, and he groans weakly until he passes out.

"Got it," Joey says a moment later as she holds up a bullet. "We need to get both of them to a hospital. Mateen needs insulin and chelation. Nomar...I'm not a surgeon. Even if I were, this isn't the place to do it. But now that the bullet's out, as long as we can keep his fever down and stop the infection from getting worse, he'll make it."

Lisette holds her son, trying to get him to sip from the glass of water. "Nomar," she says quietly, "saved my life. He picked up Mateen, and told me to come with him if I wanted to live."

"Seriously? He pulled a *Terminator* on you?" Offering the frightened woman an apologetic look when her dark brows draw together, I hold out my hand. "Sorry. It's...a movie thing. I'm Ford. Joey's...um..." *Fuck.*

"Fiancé," she says as she presses a gauze pad to Nomar's side.

The word settles me in a way I never expected, and for a single minute, I'm the happiest man in the world. But then Nomar moans, and Joey meets my gaze. "We have to go, Ford. Now. Or we might lose both of them."

17

Joey

LESS THAN TEN MINUTES LATER, we pile into the Jeep. Trevor's behind the wheel, Lisette holds Mateen in the passenger seat, and Ford and I are in the back with Nomar sandwiched between us. His breathing's labored, and infection's already set in, so he's burning up. At least I got the bullet out, but the way I did it? I worry I made things worse.

Even though I know I'm not to blame, that Faruk was the one who chose to kidnap me, who chose not to give his son the bone marrow transplant he desperately needed, I still feel responsible.

Ford keeps pressure on Nomar's wound, and Lisette rocks her son gently. The headscarf I had to put on feels like it's choking me, and I can't breathe.

"Joey, buttercup, look at me." Ford's command draws me out of my panic, and I meet his gaze over Nomar's head. The wounded soldier's no more than five-foot-eight. "Remember what we discussed. If anyone stops us, you're—"

"Esin. I'm your wife, and this is your cousin. I know." Trevor handed out cover stories—apparently what he'd been working on all night long—though we don't have one for Lisette or Mateen, and if we're stopped, I don't think cover stories are going to matter much for any of us.

"Amir Abdul Faruk is one of the most powerful tribal leaders in this region," Trevor says from behind the wheel. "We can't use the border crossings. Especially with Nomar and Mateen."

"So, we're trapped in Afghanistan?" I ask.

"Hell, no. We just can't use a border crossing. We're going to find a way across the river. But we can't do that until it gets dark. For now, there's a small rural medical clinic twenty minutes east. It's, in part, run by NATO, and they'll look the other way when we show up. Joey, can you stabilize Nomar and Mateen for twelve to fifteen hours? I should be able to work some magic with the border patrols and get us across around 3:00 a.m."

"Maybe?" Against me, Nomar shudders, and more blood seeps from between Ford's fingers. "But if we don't get there soon..." I don't want to say the words. Nomar's too close to death. And right now, I need him to fight.

Trevor meets my gaze in the rearview mirror and nods. "Got it. Once we get out of the city, I can floor it. Until then...we have to try to stay under the radar."

BY THE TIME we reach the clinic, Nomar's pulse is thready and weak, and his breathing shallow. If he lasts another hour, it'll be a miracle. I can't pull myself out of my own head. Every time I inhale, the scent of blood mixed with the sickly sweet odor that marks Mateen's kidneys shutting down remind me of my time in that disgusting train car.

Ford keeps trying to talk to me, but I give him one-word

answers at best. Clutching Nomar's hand, I squeeze as hard as I can. "Stay with me," I murmur. His eyelids flutter, but he doesn't otherwise respond.

"Don't get out of the car," Trevor orders as he throws the Jeep into park and heads for the small, squat building with rough-hewn sand-colored walls and a door that looks to have been kicked in more than once.

He disappears inside, and Ford pulls his gun from the holster, hops out of the Jeep, and puts his back to the door. Mateen says something to Lisette in Pashto, and she coos quietly to him. "It will be okay, my son. Dr. Joey will help you."

"Mama, are we going back to Papa soon?" Mateen sounds so desperate, and Lisette shakes her head.

"Shhh. We will speak of that later," she whispers. "For now, we must be quiet and not say Papa's name. Do you understand?"

"Yes, Mama." He turns his face into Lisette's shoulder and sighs.

How can a man who claims to love his family do so much to hurt them? Shifting slightly, I check Nomar's pulse again. Lisette turns in her seat to meet my gaze. "Will he live?"

"I don't know." He's beyond hearing me now. But saying the words still brings a lump to my throat and my eyes start to burn. So much death, and I just wanted to help people.

"He risked his life for me and my son. If he needs blood, I am type O. I will donate to him."

I offer her a grateful smile, and as Trevor comes jogging out of the clinic, a small spark of hope flares to life. Maybe...we won't be too late.

Ford

This room gets smaller the longer we stay here. Joey's sitting on the floor, her back against the wall between two cots, Mateen on one, and Nomar on the other. She managed to get both of them stabilized, but it was touch and go. During the transfusion, she lost Nomar's heartbeat for a full minute, and I kept up chest compressions until she found it again.

She fell asleep an hour ago, but she's restless. Her lips twist into a frown, and behind her lids, her eyes move rapidly. I'm on watch since Trevor never ended up getting any shuteye. The rural doctor who runs this clinic agreed to hide us—once we handed over two thousand dollars, and we have at least another three hours before it's safe enough for us to head to the river crossing.

Dax called in a favor—more than one—and arranged for a medical transport chopper to pick us up in Termez and fly us to Qarshi. Once we're there, I'll be able to breathe again. Maybe. Now that we've taken his wife, and more importantly, his son, Faruk is sure to come after us. Trev called Matt as soon as we arrived, and once we get to Qarshi, we'll be protected. False IDs for Mateen and Lisette, a JSOC safehouse for Trev, me, and Joey, and secure transport back to the States. Hell, he even found Lisette's family and got in touch with her sister.

"Nnnnoooo," Joey whimpers, "no, no, no..." Tears stream down her cheeks, and before I can get to her, she lets out a wail, waking Trevor and Lisette, both sleeping in chairs in the corners of the room.

"Joey!" I catch her as she's about to fall over, and her entire body goes stiff in my arms. Wild, terrified eyes scan the room. Trev's on his feet, his Glock in his hand. Lisette immediately goes to Mateen's side, but then returns to her chair as she realizes what's going on.

Straining against me, Joey whimpers again, and I tighten my embrace. "It's me, buttercup. You're safe."

"Ford? Oh, shit." Her cheeks turn bright red, though the yellowing bruises hide much of her blush. Searching out Trevor, she bites her lip for a moment. "I'm sorry. Go back to sleep."

He grunts what might be an "okay" and drops back into the chair.

I settle Joey against me, tucking her head under my chin. "Trev and I are going to have some serious words when we get back to the States," I whisper in her ear.

"You can't blame him." With a sniffle, she turns slightly so she can rest her head against my shoulder. "They're always...so real."

"Your nightmares?" When she nods, I continue. "Tell me?"

"Ford—"

Stroking my hand up and down her back, I press a kiss to her temple. "No secrets, remember, buttercup? I can handle it."

"I don't know if *I* can," she whispers. "For twenty years, all I've wanted...besides you...was one night where they didn't come for me. And last night," she tips her gaze up to meet mine, "I got it. My one night. It was...perfect. *You* were perfect. But what if that's all I ever get? What if that's my one good thing, and we don't make it back to Boston? What if he finds us? What if I lose you all over again?"

Her tears stream down her cheeks, tumbling from her jaw to my shirt, and she desperately tries to wipe the next wave away before they can fall. Using the edge of my sleeve, I dry her face, then kiss her—a slow, deep kiss full of promises, full of hope, full of all my love for her.

"You won't lose me." With one finger, I snag the chain she wears around her neck and pull out the ring. "Did you mean what you said back at the safe house?"

Her gaze snaps from the ring to my face and back again.

"We're different people than we were back then, Ford. We've lived a lifetime of pain, changed in ways...we could never have imagined. But...you're the only man I've ever loved. The only man I ever *want* to love. It probably won't be easy." Joey offers me a weak smile. "But I want to try."

"I can't put this back on your finger yet," I say. "Not until we're safe in Qarshi. If the guys Trev's paying to smuggle us across the river see it, they might demand you give it to them." Tucking the ring back under her shirt, I kiss her neck from her shoulder to her ear. "But soon...I will. If it's okay with you."

A single, fat tear hits her cheek, and her lips curve into a wide smile. "I'd like that. Very much."

18

Ford

THE BOAT GLIDES across the smooth surface of the river, with only a gentle breeze stirring the edges of Joey's headscarf. She leans against me, her eyes closed, as Trevor and the local he hired steer towards Uzbekistan.

The forty-minute drive from the clinic had us all on edge—except Nomar. Joey gave him a sedative before we moved him because he was in too much pain to lie still. But now, with Afghanistan behind us, I start to relax.

We're going home. In a roundabout way. Qarshi, then Adana, Turkey, and then back to Boston. Joey keeps flexing her fingers like she wants to dig her nails into her palms, but each time I'm about to stop her, she blows out a slow, even breath and relaxes.

I have so many questions for her. So many things I need to know. Likes and dislikes. Does she still hate peas? What's her favorite movie? Pizza or fried chicken? Summer or winter? I used to know all the answers. Now...?

"Mama," Mateen whines, and Lisette claps her hand over his mouth.

"Shhh, my son. It is important to be quiet now," she hisses. Glancing my way, she looks so ashamed, but he's a kid. Hell, I'm surprised he hasn't had a meltdown.

The boat jerks as our guide directs it onto the sandy riverbank, then hops out, grabs the bow, and along with Trevor, drags the boat up far enough up the shore that the rest of us can get out without landing in knee-deep water.

It takes both me and Trevor to haul Nomar's unconscious ass out of the boat and get him into the back of an SUV. After another cash payment—the last five thousand dollars I have on me—the man hands over the keys.

"Well," Trevor says as he pulls the vehicle onto the main road, "we made it. Another hour and we'll be somewhere Faruk can't touch any of us again."

I hope to God he's right.

Joey wraps her arms around me and buries her face against my neck. Her quiet sobs make me want to rip Faruk's balls off and force them down his throat, but I'll settle for him never touching Joey again.

Joey

The apartment complex looks new, and Ford holds my hand as he leads me up a set of stairs to the second floor. "JSOC—Joint Special Operations Command—owns this entire building," he says quietly. "It's swept for bugs daily. No cameras except at the entrances."

He's trying to reassure me, but I'm not sure there's anything he could say to get me to relax right now. The doctors at the Qarshi hospital were able to stabilize Mateen's kidneys after several hours of fluids, and a quick session with the blood chelation machine sent his iron levels back to something close to normal. He's still a very sick boy, but at least for right now, he's resting comfortably.

"I wish they had let us see Nomar," I admit as Ford stops in front of Unit 201.

"Trev's still there. And three of Nomar's buddies are on their way. He'll hate all the fuss." Ford knocks on the door, a series of five light raps, followed by three heavier, and two light again.

I'm about to ask him what's going on when the door opens and a handsome man with jet black hair peers down at me. "So you're Joey," he says with a smile and a thick British accent. "I'm Matt. And I've been hearing stories about you for three days. Come on in."

Before I can turn to Ford, I hear Ivy.

"Oh, my God." I push my way into the room, and she practically knocks me over as she throws her arms around me. We stay locked together for a full minute, until Mia clears her throat.

"Um, can I get in on this hugging action too?"

She looks like she's been through hell. A bruise on her cheek has faded to a sickly swirl of yellow and green, and a heavy cast surrounds her right arm. But it's the look in her eyes I know all too well that breaks my heart.

"Mia, I'm so sorry." My tears make everything in the room shimmer, and as we hold on to one another, I remember how it felt to have my sister hold me that first week I was free. "I'm sorry," I say again, knowing if I apologize every day for the rest of my life, it won't be enough.

The slight young woman shakes in my embrace, and I let her cry, only moving when Ivy takes my arm and urges both of us over to the couch across the room. "We're going home in the morning," Mia says quietly after she wipes her cheeks. "Matt wanted to take us today, but when he said you'd be here tonight, we begged him to wait."

Ford sidles up to my elbow and drops down to one knee. "Matt, Leo, and I will be just outside in the hall. Take as long as you need. You're all safe here."

I cup his cheek, unsure when his stubble turned into a full beard. "You did this. All of this. Thank you."

ALMOST TWO HOURS LATER, I hug Ivy and Mia goodbye. "You can call me any time," I say, trying to keep my voice from cracking. Just before I slip into the hall, I look back at Mia. "You'll never forget. But this doesn't have to rule your entire life. Not unless you let it. Don't make the same mistake I did. Not everyone gets a second chance."

"Joey?" Mia says as she dabs her eyes with a tissue. "I'm glad you found yours."

"Me too." And when I step into Ford's embrace, I know exactly what I need from him tonight.

I want that ring back on my finger.

Ford

We're finally alone. Joey's quiet as I open the door for her. "There are guards on patrol twenty-four-seven," I say, flipping on the light. The space is small. Only a couch and a round table in the main room, a kitchenette, and a single bedroom and bath. But for the next twelve hours or so, it's all ours.

"Trev has his own place down the hall, and the building's concierge went out and picked up a few more things for us."

"The concierge?" Her brows furrow, and I dip my head to kiss the tiny line between them, smoothing it away.

"They use this place for all sorts of things. Visiting military brass, vetted asylum seekers waiting for relocation, government assets... If there's anything else you need before we get on the plane tomorrow night, just ask."

The look on her face...I want to give her the world. Every single thing she's ever desired laid out on a platter.

"I just need you. And a shower. And maybe some fresh clothes. And dinner." She stifles her laugh against my shoulder, and when she gets herself under control and draws back, her smile makes me feel like the only man in the world. "Okay," she says. "I guess I need a lot of things."

"As you wish." I offer her an exaggerated bow, then point her towards the bedroom. "What first?"

"Shower."

At the bedroom door, I stop, unsure where our boundaries are. Yes, we had sex. But under blankets. In dim lighting. After a very emotional reconnection. I don't want to overwhelm her or crowd her or make her at all uncomfortable. We've come so far in the past couple of days, and if I lost her now because I made a stupid assumption or couldn't keep my dick in my pants, I'd never forgive myself.

Joey drops to her knees and unzips the small suitcase at the foot of the bed with all the things I asked the government concierge to get for her—for us. "Oh," she says with a breathy sigh, and lifts the silky red bra by its straps. "Wait." She pins me with a hard stare. "You gave the concierge a list that included a red silk bra?"

"Would black have been better?"

"Ford. Be serious." Digging through the rest of the small stash, she comes up with the matching panties, a pair of soft yoga pants, pajamas, various toiletries, including razors for both of us, a new box of condoms, and a small bottle of bubble bath. "There's...a bathtub?"

Scrambling to her feet, she races into the bathroom. "Forget about food, sleep, all of it. I just want a bath."

As the water starts to splash into the tub, I back out of the room. She's not ready for me to be in there with her, even though it's the only place I want to be. "You take some time alone, buttercup. I'll handle dinner."

Joey peeks out from behind the half-closed door. "Ford?"

"I won't leave, Joey. I promise."

"I know. That's not what I wanted to say." Her full lips pull into a frown, and conflict churns in her eyes. "Don't give up on me. I'll...get there."

With a nod, I close the bedroom door. That's enough. For tonight, that's all I need.

Joey

Sinking into the hot water and bubbles, I refuse to look down at my naked skin. I should be braver. Ford loves me the way I am, but despite what I told Ivy and Mia, despite *knowing* I want to be with Ford for the rest of my life, I still see myself as that broken, scarred, damaged woman who never fully escaped a twenty-year-old nightmare.

Under the thick layer of bubbles, I slide my hands down over my breasts. My nipples send little zings of pleasure down to my core, and I jerk, splashing a few drops of water over the side of the tub.

As I move lower, close to my mound, the still-unfamiliar warmth gathers inside me. When I felt the rush of wetness between my thighs last night, I wanted to cry. I never thought I'd ever be able to be aroused again.

"I'm not broken." I try the words, seeing how they feel rolling off my tongue. Not right. But also not wrong. Maybe... maybe broken isn't the worst thing a person can be.

"You have to realize you're worthy of love, Joey." My very first therapist tried to drill that into me, over and over again. She didn't understand why I couldn't reach out to the man I had planned to marry. Every time she told me I still deserved to be loved, I'd show her my arms. The cuts...some smooth and thin, others deeper, thicker, almost jagged...that marked me as ugly. That forced me to hide who I really was. Who I'd become.

Swirling one finger between my lower lips, I let my eyes drift closed. I'm wet for him, and he's not even in the room. He'll kiss me tonight, and we'll open that new box of condoms. And maybe I'll work up the courage to ask him to put the ring back on my finger, and I'll find another piece of me I thought had been lost forever.

Ford

Joey emerges from the bedroom, her hair damp, dressed in black yoga pants and a green t-shirt. Other than fresh bandages, her feet are bare, and some of the lines of strain I thought might be permanent have faded from around her eyes and lips.

"That smells amazing. What is it?"

Taking a quick peek in the small toaster oven, I shake my head. "It's a secret. For another twenty minutes. But I have something for you to do in the meantime."

"What?" Her smile almost feels easy, unforced, like she's actually happy. But I don't know this new Joey well enough to be sure. Not yet.

Holding out my hand, I lead her over to the small couch. "I

need to clean up while dinner's cooking. And I thought that would give you a few minutes to talk to your family."

From the side of the couch, I pull out a laptop, open it, and bring up the secured video chat window. Joey lets out a sob and throws her arms around me. We stay locked together until she takes a deep, shuddering breath, and then pulls back. "Thank you. It's really safe?"

Sliding my fingers into her hair, I brush my lips to hers. "It's safe. This is Wren's encrypted connection. Nothing can break through. Don't tell them what city you're in, but the country's fine. And you can tell them you'll be back in Boston in a couple of days. Or...if you want me to arrange for a flight to San Diego for you instead, I can do that."

My heart bangs against my ribs like it's about to explode. I didn't think until now that she might want to go back to San Diego. For a visit...or for good.

"If...I wanted to go to California...would you...go with me?" If I weren't looking right at her, I wouldn't have heard her. Uncertainty swims in her eyes, and she dashes away the last remaining tear as she straightens her shoulders, almost like she's steeling herself for the answer.

"I'll go anywhere with you. All you have to do is ask."

She nods, twines our fingers, and brings our joined hands to her heart. "I love you, Ford. Right now, I just want to go home with you."

Rising, I kiss her knuckles before letting her go. "As you wish."

19

Joey

MOM AND GERRY hold on to one another and cry as I tell them I'm okay, that I was taken because of my medical knowledge. That no one violated me, that other than some bruises, I'm fine.

"You look...different," Gerry says as she sends Mom away for the last couple minutes of the call. "Not that you've come home all that often, but..."

I shoot her a look—the one that says "stop mothering me and just be my friend"—and glance back at the closed bedroom door.

"I was so stupid, Gerry." Tugging on the chain around my neck, I pull out the ring and turn it over in my palm. "I let Ford think it was all his fault for twenty years. When really, I never wanted to admit the truth."

"Which is...?"

"I was ashamed. I lost myself. And once I was lost, I couldn't find my way back." The urge to use my fingernail to trace a hard line down my inner arm prickles over my skin, but I repeat the mantra my therapist gave me years ago. *Let yourself feel.* "There's so much I never told you and Mom. Most of it...isn't important. Details I don't want to relive. But some of the rest of it... Maybe you could come visit in a month or two? I don't know where I'll be...where I'll be living...but we'll figure it out. I don't want to hide anymore."

Gerry's focus shifts to something over my shoulder, and I tense until Ford clears his throat, then once I meet his gaze, heads for the kitchen. Something in his eyes worries me. Like he's closed himself off from me, and I almost get up before I remember Gerry's still on screen, staring at me.

"Say you'll come?" I ask.

"You name the time and place, and I'll be there, sis. I love you."

"Love you too."

As much as I needed to talk to both of them, whatever has Ford's shoulders hiked up around his ears is more important. It only takes me five steps to make it to the kitchen, and I lean against the counter until he pulls a small foil tray of something cheesy and bubbly from the small toaster oven. "Lasagna? You found lasagna in Uzbekistan?"

"Yep. Take a seat." He carries the steaming tray to the small table, then returns to the kitchen for silverware, two small glasses, and a can of Coca-Cola. "I figured this might make you feel more...like you were home."

I blink hard, willing myself not to cry. "Only if you let me spill that all over you." Offering him what feels like my first genuine smile in years, I'm confused when he barely reacts. "What's wrong?"

"Just been a long day." Scooping a generous helping of lasagna onto my plate, he hardly spares me a glance, then almost immediately starts digging into his own serving. Except, after his first bite, he doesn't do more than push the noodles around on his plate.

I set my fork down, pick up my glass of soda, and stand. "If you don't tell me why you're suddenly acting like we're strangers, I *will* pour this over your head."

Shoving away from the table, Ford stalks to the single window in the living room and glances outside through a small crack in the drapes. "I love you, Joey."

Curling my fingers around his arm, I tug him towards me. "Isn't that a *good* thing? I love you, too."

"I lost you for twenty years." His eyes shine as he searches my face. "I don't ever want to lose you again. But I don't know where we stand. Are you planning to leave Boston...without me?"

"What? No!" I take a step back, needing a little space between us so I don't have to crane my neck to look into his eyes. "What gave you that idea?"

"You told Gerry you didn't know where you'd be in a month."

For a moment, I don't respond, but when I do, I start laughing. And then...it's like I can't stop. I don't remember the last time I laughed. Just...laughed. Ford's looking at me like I've lost my mind, and tears stream down my cheeks. But for the first time in weeks, maybe months, I'm not crying because I'm in pain.

Ford guides me over to the couch, his arm around my shoulders. "I'm...shit...I'm sorry," I gasp as I swipe at my cheeks and try to regain some small shred of control. Reaching back, I unclasp the chain I've worn for twenty years and pull off the ring. "When I said I didn't know where I'd be, I just meant... well...my apartment's really small. I thought maybe...we'd be living somewhere together."

He looks at me like I've just given him the answers to all the world's problems. "Together?"

"Yes, Marine. Together. Isn't that what usually happens when two people get married? You *did* ask me last night. Pretty sure I didn't imagine that." For the first time since the FBI gave the ring back to me, I press it into his hand then...let go. "But since you didn't do it properly...with this...ask me again."

Dropping to one knee, Ford stares at the diamond and sapphire band, then blows out a breath.

"Joey? I gave you my heart more than twenty years ago. Since then, I've thought about you every single day. Is she happy? Is she safe? Does she ever think about me?" He reaches for my hand, his thumb skating over my bare ring finger. "We lost so much time. But I want to make up for every second. Will you marry me?"

"The memory of the morning you proposed on the beach?" I whisper, struggling not to cry, "That was my touchstone. I'd replay that memory over and over again in my head. I'd never been so happy, and I didn't think I'd ever be that happy again. I was wrong."

"Is that a yes?" Ford arches a brow, his lips curved into the smile I dreamed of every night.

"Yes. Absolutely, yes."

Ford

Awkwardness seeps in again as we stand on opposite sides of the bed. The long-sleeved t-shirt clings to the softness of her breasts, and I don't know if she wants me to hold her, make love to her, or something in between.

"It won't always be this way, will it?" Joey asks as she practically dives under the covers. "We'll find our...normal?"

"We will." Torn between wanting to show her all of me and fearing I'll overwhelm her, I settle for stripping down to my briefs with my back to her.

"Stop," she whispers before I can slip under the covers. "Turn around."

Pushing up to her knees, she crawls over to me, wrapping a hand around each of my hips. "I want to see you."

The briefs catch on my suddenly raging hard-on, and Joey blushes crimson before she manages to free my dick and the material falls to the floor. A muscle in her jaw works back and forth, and I cup her cheek to urge her gaze to mine. "You're amazing, buttercup. But I don't need anything but you in my arms tonight."

"I do." Tentatively, she wraps her fingers around my shaft, stroking the silky skin until a drop of precum glistens at the tip. "We used to..."

"New beginnings. We don't need to do anything we *used* to do." Gently taking her elbows, I try to urge her higher so I can kiss her, but she resists. Her grip on my waist is so tight, she might actually leave a bruise. After she squeezes her eyes shut for a long blink, she opens them, gaze fixed on my dick, and leans forward to suck just my crown into her mouth. After one swirl of her tongue, she draws back and lets me pull her into my arms.

As I claim her mouth, I taste myself on her tongue, but under that, it's all Joey. The woman who agreed to marry me —twice.

"Thank you," she manages when we come up for air. "I didn't know if I could ever do that again. And...I still don't know if I can give you more—"

"I don't need more. I just need you." Scooping her up against my chest, I carry her back to the other side of the bed where the blankets are already pulled back, then climb in with her still in my arms. "I'll be here for you forever, Joey. Whatever you need. Whatever you want to try. Whatever you don't."

"Undress me." Her half-hooded eyes churn the deepest of blues, and she wriggles off my lap to stand in front of me, just like I did with her.

"Baby?" Wrapping an arm around her lower back as I swing

my legs over the side of the bed, I wait for her to meet my gaze. "Promise me something."

"What?"

"If anything makes you uncomfortable or nervous or scared, say 'stop,' okay?"

Her lips twitch into what might be a weak smile. "Ford? Are you trying to give me a safe word?"

Chuckling, I slip my fingers under her shirt so my palm rests against the warmth of her skin. "Maybe."

Her eyes shine as she dips her head and kisses me. Feather light, almost chaste, it still makes me want to bury myself balls-deep inside her. But I start with her shirt. Lifting the hem a few inches, I kiss along her stomach. Her curves, mostly hidden under her clothes, have haunted my dreams. She's still too thin, and I'll get her favorite foods every single day once we're home, but for now, I ease the shirt higher, exposing the red satin bra.

"More?" I ask, and she nods, so I strip the shirt off completely and drop it to the floor. A flush starts between her breasts, slowly spreading up her neck as I skate my thumbs over her nipples. Under the satin, hard nubs rise to meet me, and she shudders, tipping her head back and closing her eyes.

Whatever happens, she's going to know who's touching her, who's loving her. "Joey, look at me. Always at me."

Her little gasp makes my cock twitch, and seeing her respond to me, the fine hairs on her arms standing as goose-bumps cover her skin, is a gift I'll never take for granted again.

Keeping my eyes on hers, I pinch first one nipple, then the other, rolling them between my fingers until her breath is coming in short pants and a light dew breaks out over her skin.

The muscles of her stomach quiver when I reach for the waistband of her pants, and I hold her gaze. "We can stop..."

"No. I...want...this."

Careful to leave the red panties in place, I ease the pants down her hips, and the scent of her arousal wraps around me, so sweet and uniquely *Joey* that it's like we're still in our twenties and about to have sex for the very first time.

"You're beautiful, Joey. All my memories...they can't compare to what's right in front of me." With my index finger, I trace the edge of the satin, all the way from her hip to the apex of her thighs, and she whimpers quietly, her hands clutching my shoulders.

Her eyes darken. "Please..."

"Please what, baby?" I ache for her, but if she's not ready, I'll wait forever.

"T-touch me."

Slick heat welcomes me as I ease the material to the side. So wet. So soft. Her sensitive nub hardens under my touch, and after a single pass over her clit, I suck her arousal from my finger.

"More?" I ask as I wrap my arms around her.

Reaching behind her, she releases the catch on her bra, and I slide the straps off her shoulders. When her panties hit the floor, she steps back, clenching and unclenching her hands, her arms straight at her sides, her gaze on me. "You...make me feel...like I'm not completely broken."

"We're all broken, Joey." Holding out my hand, I wait for her to place her fingers in mine. In the light from the bedside lamp, the ring on her finger sparkles. "But broken isn't worthless. It's beautiful."

When she crushes her lips to mine, I sweep her into my arms, lay her down on the bed, and show her just how beautiful she is.

20

Joey

I'M NAKED. With Ford curled around me, his chest to my back. *He's behind me. And I'm okay.* He left the light on. All night. Like he has every night since he rescued me. I didn't even need to ask.

Reaching for my ring, I panic for a second until I remember it's back where it belongs. On my finger. And today, we're going home. To Boston where...we'll be together.

With my fingernail, I drag a light scratch along my forearm. Not enough to make me bleed. Not even enough to raise a welt. Just enough to confirm this isn't a dream.

"Joey?" Ford's voice is thick with sleep, and he pushes up on an elbow, gently wrapping his big hand around mine. "What's wrong?"

"Nothing." He starts to protest, but I wriggle around to face him. "That's the truth, Ford. I...needed to know this wasn't a dream."

His hazel eyes hold so many emotions: concern, love, fear,

relief...all swirling around in their depths. "We never talked about when I need to worry..." He skims his fingers over my scars. "If I'm ever the cause—"

"If it gets serious again...you'll know." I cup his cheek, the light stubble tickling my palm. "I'll tell you. But sometimes, like right now, it's just a way for me to know I'm...alive. Safe. I won't promise you I'll never cut myself again. But I'll tell you if I do."

He nods, my explanation enough for him—at least for now —and I snuggle closer.

"Maybe in a few weeks...you can come to one of my therapy sessions. Dr. Rita would probably love to meet you. God knows she's heard enough about you." I smile against his chest, and he strokes up and down my back. "She can give you some of the signs I might miss in my own behavior."

"Whatever you need, Joey. There's nothing I wouldn't do for you." His voice rumbles under my ear, and I relax into his embrace. This is a dream. The perfect dream. And maybe...for once...it doesn't have to end.

THE APARTMENT PHONE rings as I'm pulling my hair up into a messy bun. Qarshi is a large enough city I don't have to cover my head out in public, and the freedom makes me giddy.

"Joey?" Ford holds out the phone. "It's Lisette." When I draw in a sharp breath, he quickly adds, "It's good news."

"Lisette? What is it?"

"My sister...Noele," she says with such joy in her voice, I can't help my smile. "She arrived last night, and...Dr. Joey, she is a match for Mateen's bone marrow. She demanded to be tested as soon as I told her about his condition."

"Oh, my God. That's so wonderful, Lisette." Tears gather in the corners of my eyes, and I turn to Ford. "Do we have time to stop by the hospital to see Mateen and Lisette before we go?"

"Dax arranged this plane, buttercup. It'll wait for us as long as we need." He shoves the last of our clothes in his duffel bag, then takes the metal tin he used to protect his letters to me, wraps a rubber band around it, and lovingly places it on top of the bag. "We can be at the hospital in under an hour."

In the background, I hear the boy call for his mother. "I am sorry, Dr. Joey, I must go, but you will come?"

"We'll be there soon."

THE LIGHT LINEN pants billow around my legs, and though my blouse has a high neck and long sleeves, it flares at the waist, the style so very different from everything I was forced to wear when I was under Faruk's control. The SUV—with bulletproof windows and reinforced siding—carries us slowly down the Qarshi streets. For a small city, it's surprisingly congested.

Ford keeps hold of my hand, absently stroking his thumb over my engagement ring. Even though the two men in the front seat are heavily armed, he never stops checking all around us, and I lean closer to whisper in his ear. "You're worried. Why?"

Turning, he brushes a tender kiss to my lips. "Not worried. Prepared." Patting the gun strapped to his hip, he returns his gaze out the side window. "I won't take a chance with your safety. Wren's monitoring for any chatter that mentions you or Faruk, and we're getting Lisette and Mateen out of the country as soon as the kid can travel."

"You think he's going to come after his son. And once he has his son back...he'll need me again." A cold weight settles over my chest, and my throat tightens. "Ford, you can't keep things like this from me."

A muscle in his jaw ticks, and he closes his eyes for a brief moment. "It's my job to protect you. From everything."

The words he doesn't say echo in my mind, and anger prickles along my skin. "Including from myself. That's what you're really saying, isn't it? That you didn't trust me with your concerns because you thought I'd cut myself again. That I wouldn't be able to handle it."

"Joey—"

Yanking my hand away from his, I shake my head. "Don't 'Joey' me. I've spent the last twenty years of my life alone. I put myself through school, paid off all my student loans, made a name for myself in the medical community." My voice breaks, and I blow out a slow, controlled breath to rein in my emotions. "I have nightmares, Ford. I can't sleep in the dark. Men...almost all men...scare the crap out of me. And yes. When things are at their worst, I self-harm. But if you want this to work, you have to *trust* me."

The car is deathly silent, our two escorts keeping their heads pointed straight ahead as we make the turn into the hospital parking lot. When Alec, the burlier of the two, opens the back door for me, I give Ford's profile a hard stare. "I'm going to see Lisette and Mateen. Are you coming? Or not?"

His swallow is audible, even over the hum of the traffic down the street. "I have to check in with Nomar. Get the video he recorded of Faruk's compound for Wren. Alec and Jackson won't let you out of their sight. I'll be there in a few minutes. Take this with you." He hands me a folding knife, and I shove it into my pocket.

"Fine." As I get to my feet, I square my shoulders. "We're not done with this conversation. I love you, Ford. With everything I am. You saved my life. More than that...I think you saved a part of who I used to be. Who I was meant to be all along. A part of me I didn't know was still locked deep inside. But those words I said all those years ago? They're still true. This doesn't work if you don't trust me."

Ford

I'm in a foul mood when I shove through the door to Nomar's room. Wires and tubes snake from underneath the drab hospital gown, and he's paler than I've ever seen him. But he turns his head and gives me a weak grin as I drop into the chair next to him. "'Bout time, asshole."

"You were unconscious last time I checked. Cut me some fucking slack." Despite the harshness of my words, there's no animosity between us.

"Listen," he says, his voice raspy. "I'm sorry I put everyone in danger by grabbing Lisette and the kid."

"I would have done the same thing." Flopping back in the chair, I run both hands over my hair and down my neck. Tension turns my shoulders to granite, and I can't wait to get out of Uzbekistan and back to the States where I can hire some private security for Joey until we know Faruk is no longer a threat. "You have the video surveillance you took of the compound? Wren wants to pull any face she can find and run it through her software. She'll watch the airports—both here and in France—for any sign Faruk's on the move and coming after his son or Joey."

He nods and presses a button on the bed's remote to raise himself up slightly. "My bag's hidden under the corner of the mattress. Get it for me?"

Only a spook—or former spook—would go to such lengths in a hospital. The waterproof oilskin bag is no bigger than a book, and Nomar uses one hand to unzip it and withdraw a small data card. "This should have everything you need. Video from my initial recon and from the night we broke Joey out."

"Thanks, man. When they letting you out of here?" I'm

itching to go check on Joey, but she's right. I need to trust her. She has two lethal bodyguards with her, Lisette and Mateen are using forged papers—courtesy of Matt and his guys—and security patrols the halls regularly. Hell, there's a guard stationed not more than twenty feet from the kid's room.

Nomar shifts, a wince flattening his lips. "Three or four days. Listen, you think there might be some work for me at Second Sight when I'm healed up? Never gave much thought to what I'd do after this. But...seeing Lisette's face when I told her I was taking her with me..." He rubs his chin, a faraway look in his eyes for a moment. "I want to help people, Ford. I just don't want to do it in this part of the world anymore."

Reaching out, I clap Nomar gently on the shoulder. "Normally, I'd run a new hire by Dax. But pretty sure he'd be thrilled to have you join the team. Call me when you get back to the States, and we'll make it official."

Joey

Alec leads the way, but Jackson insists on walking behind me. I keep looking over my shoulder, my heart hammering against my ribs. Some days, I feel like I've beaten my demons. Others, they follow me everywhere.

My conversation with Ford plays on a loop in my head. I know he loves me. He's not wrong. If I'd known about the danger this whole time, I might have been more tempted to cut myself. Or simply shut down. But he's also not right either. We lost one another once because we were both too stubborn to open up. I won't let that happen again.

At the door to Mateen's room, I stop. "That little boy and his mom have been through hell. Can you both please wait outside?"

"No, ma'am. We have our orders," Alec says as he reaches for the door handle.

"It's a tiny room. With one window that doesn't open. How about a compromise. You verify there's no threat and *then* wait outside?" My entire body relaxes when Alec agrees, and after a quick sweep of the small room and even smaller bath, he emerges into the hall and stares down at me, one brow cocked.

"If *anything* seems out of place, you scream. Understood?"

"Loud enough to be heard in the next town. Understood."

LISETTE WRAPS her arms around me as soon as I walk into the room. Her hair is loose and long, dark locks flowing over her slim shoulders, and she wears jeans and a pretty floral blouse with a decidedly Western style. "I am so happy you could come," she says as she releases me. "This is my sister, Noele."

A younger woman, no older than twenty-five, embraces me and kisses both cheeks. "I owe you a debt I can never repay. Ten years we searched, and we had given up hope. Mama and Papa cannot wait to meet their grandson."

"You don't owe me anything. Except maybe pictures once in a while? Of Mateen growing up big and strong?"

Noele and I exchange email addresses, and I slide a hip onto the edge of Mateen's bed. He's playing FIFA again, and I peer at the screen. "Who's winning?"

"I am! Want to play?" His eyes are bright and clear, though he looks so frail in the big bed. A machine beeps twice, and I glance over at the monitor. His blood glucose is still over two hundred—not deadly, but way too high—and with a tiny hiss, the screen confirms the delivery of a small dose of fast-acting insulin through the pump.

"Okay, kiddo. One game, and then I have to go."

He pouts, but not more than two minutes into our match,

he's giggling as I try to make one of my electronic players head-butt the ball, but instead, send him sprawling face first onto the pitch.

Noele excuses herself to get some coffee from the hospital cafeteria, and Lisette curls up in a chair next to Mateen's bed, letting her eyes drift close. She's been through hell, and I can't imagine what it's like fearing for your child's life. My attention wanders to the window where a flash of light from a building across the street distracts me long enough for Mateen to score the final goal. He cheers as the door bangs open, and when I turn, my heart stops, and I'm too scared to scream.

Dr. Simms—Mateen's endocrinologist—falls to the floor as Zaman, dressed in scrubs and now clean-shaven, slams the butt of his pistol into the kind, older man's head. Blood streams from the wound, and I try to scream, but no sound comes out.

"I know there are American security personnel in the hall," Zaman says, his voice low and even. "If you alert them, I will kill the doctor. And we will wait right here for your sister to return, and I will have my way with her."

No. "You are not going to hurt them again," I say with more bravado than I feel.

Zaman's hand flies, and as the gun connects with my cheek, pain explodes over my entire face, the world going dark and fuzzy, with tiny pinpricks of bright light scattered across my field of vision.

Sliding to the floor, I curl inward, desperate to protect myself from any more blows. Lisette's voice echoes, like she's far away, or under water. "We will not go back with you. My son will not become like his father."

She screams as Zaman yanks her against him, but the sound fades when he wraps his hand around her throat. "Amir Faruk was very clear. The boy and the doctor. You are...expendable."

The door bangs open, Alec and Jackson rushing in, guns

drawn. "Let her go!" Alec orders, but a second later, two odd *plinks* sound, and a hint of the hot outside air blows in. The two guards go down, Alec clutching his chest, Jackson with a blackened, reddish hole where his left eye once was.

Faruk sent a sniper.

Ford. If he comes in here...

"Wait! I manage, struggling to my knees. The room spins around me, but I force myself to stagger to my feet, bracing myself against the bed for support. "I'll go with you. Me and Mateen. I won't fight or scream as long as you don't hurt Lisette. No one else has to die. Let me unhook Mateen's monitors and IV the right way. If I don't, he's not going to survive the journey back to Afghanistan."

Zaman eyes me suspiciously, his fingers still tight around Lisette's throat. She wheezes, tears streaming down her cheeks, and stares at me like I've just betrayed the most sacred of trusts. If only I could tell her I'm trying to keep all of us alive long enough to get help. At my feet, the doctor's eyelids flutter, but Zaman doesn't seem to notice, all his focus on the boy and the myriad of tubes and wires hooked up to him.

"Lisette, I'm so sorry," I whisper. "But think of Noele. She's just down the hall, remember? Visiting that man in two-four-seven? If she comes back in here..."

Understanding dawns in her eyes, and she sags against Zaman's hold. With a jerk of his head towards Mateen, he growls, "Ready him. Now. You have one minute." I glance down at the doctor's crumpled form, and he meets my gaze for a brief second, before he closes his eyes again. I hope he's smart enough to play possum until we're out of the room and then go get Ford.

My hands shake as I clamp the IV, pull it from the boy's arm, and then cup his cheek. *"Don't worry,"* I mouth. *"I won't let anything happen to you."* Out loud, I tell him, "You have to be very quiet now, Mateen. We're going for a ride. Do you understand?"

The boy's wide eyes shift from me to his mother to Zaman, and tears glisten in the corners. "I want to stay here," he whines.

"I know, baby. But trust Dr. Joey, okay?" Lisette says. Pressing buttons on two of the machines, I turn off their displays, unhook the oxygen sensor from his finger, and disconnect the heart rate monitor. *Please let this work.*

Scooping Mateen into my arms and then depositing him into the wheelchair in the corner of the room, I meet Zaman's gaze. "The way the machines work, someone will notice he's not hooked up to them soon. We have to leave right now."

He shifts his hold on Lisette, taking her by the upper arm and pressing the gun to her side. "Anyone you ask for help will die," he warns.

"I get it, asshole." I'm so very scared, but also pissed off. I was about to get my happy ever after, and Faruk and his lackeys want to steal me away. Again. I have to find a way out of this. For all of us.

We don't make it ten steps down the hall before a nurse stops us. "Where are you taking him?" she asks.

"The doctor," I nod at Zaman, "wants him to have an MRI. We're going to radiology. He didn't want to go without us." Offering the nurse a tight smile, I pray she believes me.

"But Dr. Joey—"

"Hush, Mateen. Remember what I said about these tests. They're necessary. They won't hurt a bit." Returning my gaze to the nurse, I shrug. "Kids. It has to be so hard for them to have all these procedures one after another after another."

"It is." She kneels down next to Mateen and pats his knee. "When you're done, I'll bring you some sugar-free Jell-O, okay, kiddo?"

Mateen looks up at me, as if he doesn't know what he's

allowed to say. Good boy. I answer for him, "That will be great. Thank you."

A minute later, we're in the elevator, heading down to the basement parking garage, and I'm terrified no one will ever hear from us again.

21

Ford

I'M ABOUT to say goodbye to Nomar when an alarm blares, and the door to his room opens. A man in a white doctor's coat lurches in, blood streaming from his temple. "Two-four-seven... The American woman said...to come here."

The American woman? Joey. Fuck.

I spring to my feet and grab the doctor by his arms to keep him upright. "What happened?"

"A man...he had a gun. Made me bring him into the little boy's room. He took them." The doctor's eyes roll back in his head, and he slumps in my grip. Easing him to the floor, I sprint out of the room, and I'm halfway into the hall when I hear Nomar's groan.

"I'm right...behind you," he manages.

I don't have the time to tell him he should keep his ass in bed. Not if Faruk and his men have Joey. Shoving through the door of Mateen's room, I skid to a stop. Alec and Jackson. Dead. Warm air swirls through the room from two small holes in the window.

Dropping into a crouch, I pull my gun just as there's a small *plink* and a bit of plaster flakes off the wall behind me. Fuck. Sniper. I crab-walk to the door just as two guards come racing down the hall. "Stay down and away from the windows," I shout as I look around wildly. Someone had to have seen them. "Where did the boy in this room go?"

A young woman who looks a lot like Lisette rushes around a corner. "Where are my sister and Mateen?"

A young nurse, no older than twenty-five, pops her head up from behind a desk. "His doctor wanted him to have an MRI. Or...that's what I thought." She points down the hall towards the elevator. "They went that way."

Shit. "Parking garage." Nomar lurches toward me, the hospital gown flapping around his bare legs. "Get the fuck back in bed," I snap, then jerk my head toward the guards. "You two. With me. And you damn well better be armed."

The taller of the two pulls a Markov from his holster and flicks off the safety. "We go first."

"No." I hit the stairwell at a run. "I'm a former United States Marine, and Faruk has my fiancé. For the second fucking time. You back *me* up. There's at least one sniper across the parking lot, and probably two men in the garage. Three hostages. Two women, and one seven-year-old boy."

Passing the first floor, I vault over the railing, clearing seven steps at once. At the door to the underground garage, I stop, twist the knob slowly, and open it just a crack.

"No!" Joey says from halfway across the structure. Her voice cracks, but remains strong. "You can't tie me up. Mateen's sick. He's going to need fluids and insulin during the trip. You have to let me take care of him. What do you think will happen if you bring Faruk his son...dead?"

The sickening sound of a fist hitting flesh masks my first few steps into the garage, and I direct the two guards to take up flanking positions. A quiet rage simmers under my skin, and I creep forward slowly, gun drawn.

"Dr. Joey!"

A muffled cry—Lisette?—follows, along with several metallic thuds. Mateen whines in rapid fire Pashto, and I peer around an ambulance. Shit. Lisette is bound and gagged in the back of a van, Mateen in a wheelchair, and Joey struggles to her feet next to him.

"Get him into the van," a large man orders, waving a gun in Joey's face. "Now."

Joey takes Mateen's arm and helps him into the vehicle where he snuggles up to his mother and touches her cheek. "Mama? Mama?"

The gunman grabs Joey by her hair and shoves her forward, but she twists in his grip and knees him in the balls. He stumbles back, the gun falling from his hand, and I rush him, firing as I go.

One shot tears through his shoulder, but my second and third shots miss him by inches. Joey dives for the gun at the same time as the asshole, and he lands on top of her. She whimpers as she struggles under his weight, and though I'm still thirty feet away, I can see her eyes go glassy. "Joey! Fight, baby!"

I can't risk hitting her with another shot, but just before I reach her, a massive weight slams into me, sending me careening into a dilapidated sedan.

"Not so fast," my attacker says, his voice deep and heavily accented. Shots echo around the garage, and angry voices shout back and forth in several different languages.

"Joey!" I have to get to her. Have to get her back. I won't lose her again. A fist slams into my ribs, then another straight to my sternum. The impact paralyzes me long enough for him to haul me to my knees and wrap his forearm around my neck.

"No..." I grunt with the last of my breath as he tightens his grip. My vision starts to dim, and all I can hear are Joey's panicked cries as she begs for her life, for her freedom.

Joey

I'm not here. Not in this underground garage. I'm back in that train car, *Jefe* on top of me, his fetid breath making me gag.

Ford's strangled cry rips me from my memories. Zaman pulls me by the hair, and my gaze lands on Ford. Oh God. He's on his knees with Full-Beard's arm around his neck, and as he struggles for breath, his body twitches and his face starts to turn blue.

No. Not Ford. Not me. Not any of us.

Faruk doesn't get to win.

Zaman has me halfway back to the van when I reach into my pocket for the folding knife Ford gave me. It springs open with a solid *snap*, and I drive it into Zaman's thigh, twisting as he lets go of my hair and I tumble to the ground.

Blood coats my hand, and I lose my grip on the knife, but the gun's only ten feet away.

As my fingers close around the barrel, Zaman grabs the waistband of my pants and yanks me back. But I have the gun, and I slam it against his temple. He roars what I think is an oath, but then he grunts and falls, and when I look up, Lisette stands over him with a tire iron.

Her wrists are still ziptied together, but the gag hangs around her neck, and she's breathing heavily. Solid footsteps pound towards us, and I whirl around with the gun just as a shot rings out from the elevator. A man with a long, lethal-looking sniper rifle collapses twenty feet away, his temple half obliterated by the bullet.

Too more shots, and I hear Nomar's weak cry. "Ford. Get...
to...Ford..."

I don't think, just run. Ford's on the ground, not moving,
and as I sink to my knees, I press my fingers to his neck. Nothing. "Ford! No!"

Rolling him onto his back, I clasp my hands one over the
other and start chest compressions. "One, two, three..." I whisper, and when I hit thirty, I tilt his head back, pinch his nose,
and blow gently into his mouth. After a second breath, I go
back to the compressions, tears streaming down my cheeks.

Thirty more, another two breaths, and I'm panicked and
half hysterical. Two hospital guards surround me, one of them
barking instructions into a radio. I'm about to breathe for him
for a third time, when Ford coughs weakly and draws in a
wheezing breath. Then another.

"Ford. Oh God, Ford, open your eyes. Look at me." Framing
his face with my hands, I lean close, touching my forehead to
his. "You're okay. You're going to be okay. Just...keep breathing."

His lips brush against mine, and though his words are
hoarse and barely audible, I hear him.

"As...you...wish..."

22

Ford

MY THROAT HURTS LIKE A MOTHERFUCKER, and the bruises Joey gave me doing CPR throb with each breath. But I'm alive. And so is she.

The EMTs load Nomar onto the first gurney. The asshole opened up half his stitches running after me, but his shot took down the sniper and the bearded son-of-a-bitch who choked me to death.

Death. The word never used to frighten me. Not truly. I've faced it before. Six times in my life—four of them in Iraq. Once on a case. Today. And all I can think is that if Joey had been a minute later, if she hadn't been able to escape the guy trying to steal her away, I'd be dead, and she'd be alone.

Blood from her temple seeps into my shirt. She's curled against my side on the dirty concrete floor, her hand over my heart when the guys in blue scrubs rush over and start to triage our various injuries.

"Get them up and onto gurneys," one of them says, but Joey tightens her hold on me.

"No. I'm...a doctor. I can walk. And I'm not leaving him."

"You have a head wound," the EMT replies. "Procedure."

"Fuck procedure." Gingerly pushing myself up on an elbow, I keep my other arm around Joey. My voice is hoarse and weak, but whatever the guy sees in my eyes convinces him to back away with his hands in the air, then wave over another guy with a wheelchair.

I feel like I got hit by a truck, and walking...probably not a smart idea. So I let them help me into the contraption, then pull Joey into my lap. "Not...letting go...of you."

She nods, and though my vision wavers a little, I think I see relief welling in her eyes. Along with a contusion the size of a grapefruit on the side of her head. Shit. We both could have—

"Don't," she whispers in my ear. "Don't even think it. You're mine, Ford Lawton. You're not allowed to die on me, and I'm certainly not going to die on you. Nothing comes between us. Ever again."

Two hours later, we're sharing a narrow hospital bed, our flight to the states delayed until Trevor gives us the all clear that the trip to the airport won't be a suicide mission.

"How did he find us?" Joey asks, then winces as she wriggles up to sitting and drops the cold pack she had pressed to her cheek on the little side table. "We were careful. Nomar got the tracker out of Lisette's clothing. Mateen didn't have one. And you said...Wren hacked the hospital records in Kandahar to make it look like they were patients there...not here."

"Don't know." Talking hurts, but I'd read her *War and Peace* if I thought it would somehow allay her fears. Problem is...I don't have any answers.

A brisk knock makes her flinch, and I push myself up with a

groan so I can wrap my arms around her as the door opens and Trevor pokes his head in. "This an okay time?"

Yelling at him? Completely worth the pain. "Where the fuck were you? Faruk's men invade the hospital and Nomar's the one who shoots the last of them?"

"I was arranging the goddamn plane. And the security to get us there. And security back in Boston when we landed. Paying off the airport officials so no one would report the flight... Shit. You want me to go back and undo all that shit so Faruk can track us all the way home?"

"Ford," Joey says quietly, "it's all right. We...made it. There's no guarantee Trevor wouldn't have gotten himself killed if he'd been here."

The logical part of my brain knows this. The part that almost died and watched the woman I love be beaten? It's not so sure. With a sigh, I gesture to the chair by the bed. "Sorry, man."

"No need. I get it. And I'm sorry." For several minutes, no one speaks, but then Trevor lets out a heavy breath. I've watched nine of my friends die," he admits as he drops a duffel bag on the floor and then sinks into the hard plastic seat. "One of them right in front of me. Another...I shot myself. Point-blank range. Didn't matter that he was a killer and a traitor. He was my best fucking friend, and I couldn't let anyone else take the shot."

This is more than Trev's talked about himself...ever.

"I'm so sorry," Joey says as she settles against me.

He shrugs. "Part of the life. I should have been here. And if things had turned out differently...I'd never have been able to forgive myself. But..." Meeting my gaze with a half-smile, he holds up Mateen's little gaming device, "I figured out how Faruk tracked us."

"Mateen loves that game. He taught me to play." Joey rubs

her swollen eye, then hisses out a breath. "You disabled the tracker, right?"

"Better than that. It's on its way back to Afghanistan on a vegetable truck. He'll probably suspect something's wrong before long when he can't reach his men, but I figure that will buy us enough time to get the fuck out of here."

"We're leaving?" I rasp. Thank God.

"As soon as you can get your sorry ass out of bed and change clothes." Trevor stands and shoves his hands into his pockets. "Matt's getting Lisette, Noele, and Matten settled in the transpo. Nomar can't fly for another three days, but he's already in an ambulance headed for Samarkand, and he'll be in Boston by the weekend." Gesturing to the duffel bag he dropped by the chair, he sighs. "Fresh clothes are in there."

"We'll be ready in ten minutes." Shoving the blanket off us, I help Joey to her feet as Trevor pauses with his hand on the door handle.

"Ford?" he says, his voice low and almost monotone, "when we get back and unpack all this shit, there are some things about me you're going to want to know. Things I should have told you a long time ago."

Joey

It feels like we've been traveling for a week, even though it's only been a little over eighteen hours. Mateen is safe at St. Jude's with a guard on his door twenty-four-seven. Courtesy of Ford and his boss, Dax, Lisette and Noele have a little apartment three blocks away and their own private security.

Midway through our travels, Ford asked me for my address, and I was so tired, I didn't even wonder why until the black

SUV, driven by his friend Clive, pulls up in front of a brownstone in Charleston.

"We're home, buttercup. At least...our temporary home." His voice is stronger now, and he holds out his hand to help me from the vehicle. Clive scans the area, then leads the way, opening Ford's apartment door and moving quickly through the space, gun drawn.

"Ronan'll be out here all night," Clive says after he declares the apartment clear. "And Wren's monitoring for chatter. We hear anything, you'll know."

"Thanks." Ford claps Clive on the back and then shuts and locks the door. The lights illuminate the masculine space, a rich leather sofa and recliner, a dark wood dining table with six chairs, the large flatscreen television.

"I'll give you the full tour later," he says as he leads me down a hall, past what looks like a home office and a bathroom, and into a large master suite. At the foot of the king-sized bed, a bench holds two suitcases. *My* suitcases.

"Ford?"

He stares down at his shoes. "I don't think there's any danger. But...I almost lost you again yesterday, Joey. I had Ella go to your place and pack...whatever she thought you'd need for the next few days."

"The next few days? *Two* suitcases? I can pack a week's worth of clothes and toiletries in a backpack." Despite my shock, the gesture makes my eyes burn, and I wrap my arms around his waist. "Thank you." Peering up at him, I frown. "What did you mean our *temporary* home?"

The corded muscles of his back flex as he shrugs. "That's up to you. This place isn't in my name. No one at Second Sight uses their real name on their leases. Safer that way. It's a nice neighborhood. Quiet. Easy access to the T. But if you want to move somewhere new...somewhere that's *ours*, then that's what we'll do."

Pulling back, Ford slides his fingers through my hair to cup the back of my neck. "I love you, Joey. We can't go back and have the life we planned out twenty years ago. But we're damn sure going to have one hell of a life together. Starting right now."

His lips crash down on mine, and suddenly, there's nothing else in my world but him. My Marine. The man I've loved for two decades. He saved me. And in the end, it was his love that helped me save myself.

EPILOGUE

Ryker

CODING MYSELF INTO OUR CONDO, I roll my head to work out the kinks in my neck. The loud crack seconds after the door opens makes Wren yelp, and she barely holds on to her laptop.

My heart skips a beat. Seeing her curled up on our couch, working, is the best sight to come home to. "Sorry, sweetheart," I say as Pixel leaps up and starts yipping and running circles around me. "Hey, furball."

Wren's smile staggers me. Every day, I wonder what she saw in my eyes when we met. "You're home."

"Damn right." I pull her into my arms, letting her wrap her legs around my waist. "Missed you."

"Obviously," she says with a laugh.

My jeans are suddenly painfully tight, and the scent of her, all that honeysuckle and heat, means we might not make it to the bedroom. "Can you take a break?"

"Almost." She lowers her head and kisses me, her tongue tracing the seam of my lips. I yield to her demands, nipping at the corner of her mouth before she pulls back. "I just got this surveillance video from Nomar of that compound where they had Ford's fiancé. I want to load it into my facial recognition software and let it run. It'll probably take all night. Or...at least long enough for us to do...other things."

As she returns to her computer, I head for the fridge for a beer. "I like the sound of that."

"Thought you would. Grab me one?" Wren's fingers fly over the keyboard. "Got a good way through unraveling Faruk's finances too. The guy's got a computer genius on his payroll. I tracked deposits through five different countries, multiple banks... He's good. But I'm better. All the trails lead back to his compound in Afghanistan. Close to Mazari Sharif."

Afghanistan. Not far from Hell. The hiss as I open the beers reminds me I'm free. Safe. With Wren in our condo in Seattle. Not back in those caves. Talking with Dax over the past ten days has brought up some painful memories, and I've been riding the edge of the darkness inside me for so long, I don't know what it's like to be on solid ground.

"Ford's back, right? They're both safe?" Dropping down next to her, I hand her the beer, then let Pixel settle in my lap. Stroking the pup's fur, I force myself to relax.

"Yep. Trevor said they got back a few hours ago." After she enters another set of commands, she makes a low, frustrated sound I've never heard her make before. Was that a...growl? "Succotash."

"Succotash?" The laugh that rolls through me eases the last of the tension behind my eyes and reminds me just how fucking lucky I am. Even if I can't keep up with all the odd words Wren uses in place of more conventional curses. "I love you, little bird."

Her fingers still on the keys, and she peers up at me, a soft smile tugging her lips and her jade green eyes dark. "I love you too. And I'm glad you're home. How was training?"

I ramble on as she works, and amazingly, she listens to

every word and still manages to follow a set of financial trans-actions from one bank to another. "Everyone seemed glad to be back after West's honeymoon."

"And you?" Searching my face, she huffs quietly. "Don't answer now. But tonight...talk to me?"

How does she know? That if I peel back the lid on the darkness, I won't be able to put it away and let her finish her work?

"I can read you, Ry. Some day, maybe it'll stop surprising you." With a quick squeeze to my thigh, she returns her focus to the laptop and shakes her head. "This is so weird," she mutters. "Every single transaction has an extra piece of code that makes no sense. It doesn't do anything. But it's obviously important. This guy's too good to put useless information in these wire transfers."

Glancing over at the screen, I choke on my sip of beer, take Wren's laptop over her sputtered protest, and stare at the string of letters and numbers I know better than my own birthdate.

94820RJT008000

In a little window off to the side of the screen, the surveillance video plays, and I pause, rewind, and zoom in.

"Holy fucking shit."

"Ry? What the heck is this?"

I can't force the word over the lump in my throat. Six years. Six years and eight months. Pulling out my phone, I send a text to my team.

HVT located in Afghanistan. We leave in three hours. Plan on being gone five days.

Within minutes, Inara, West, and Graham have all confirmed, and Wren's staring at me like I've grown a second head.

She arches her brow. "Ryker McCabe, what in the hockey pucks is going on here?"

"Pack a bag, sweetheart. We're going to Boston."

Ford

Joey's quiet whimpers rouse me, and I skim my palm up and down her arm. "Shhh, buttercup. I'm right here."

Her body relaxes, and she sighs, turning towards me and settling when her hand finds my heart. The deep purple bruises still ache, but if this means she can sleep peacefully, she can do this all day long.

For years, I fantasized about having her in my bed. In my life. And now that she's here...I wonder how we're going to find our normal.

An hour later, I'm still staring at her when her eyelids flutter, and she smiles. "Are you watching me sleep?" Joey asks lazily.

"No."

"Liar." Stretching her arms over her head, she groans. "Ow. I'm *really* looking forward to a day when I wake up without fresh bruises."

Her nipples strain against the plain blue t-shirt she wore to bed, and my dick rises to attention, tenting my pajama pants. Quickly, I turn on my side and pull the blankets up to my waist. "Tomorrow. I promise, buttercup. No one's going to bruise you today."

With a sigh, Joey sits up and runs her fingers lightly along the edge of the swelling on my chest. "I'm sorry about this. I mean...I'm not. But I am."

Twining our fingers, I bring her knuckles to my lips. "You saved my life. I think that's worth a little discomfort. Now...what do you want to do today?"

Joey laughs, then plants a kiss to my temple. "I want a cheeseburger. French fries. Maybe a beer."

"For breakfast?"

"God, no. How about we start with coffee? Then...maybe we can go to my place? Ella...she did a great job. But she didn't pack my makeup, any of my sweaters, or...my journals." Joey's eyes cloud over, turning the gray-blue of an impending storm. "And there's a box under my bed."

She looks so sad, so terribly lost, and in that moment, there's nothing I wouldn't do for her. "Joey? What's in the box?"

The corners of her mouth twitch into a smile, even as her lower lip wobbles and a tear spills onto her cheek. "Two of your t-shirts. The stuffed unicorn you won for me at the San Diego County Fair. And...our engagement photos."

Crushing her against me, I kiss her, even as she protests her morning breath. But a moment later, she straddles me, deepening the kiss, and I slide my hands down her hips to cup her ass.

"Make love to me, Ford," she says quietly. "I want to start this new life of ours...right now."

"Oh, I forgot how good it was to have conditioner," Joey says as she emerges from the bathroom wrapped in a towel, her blond locks practically shining in the morning sun.

As soon as she sees me staring at her, she turns away, but I catch the flush reddening her cheeks. By the time I cross the room, she's gripping her left forearm with her right hand hard enough the tips of her fingers turn white, but before I can say a word, she blows out a breath and meets my gaze.

"I'm sorry." Her voice is so low and quiet, I can barely hear her.

"For?" With my arm around her waist, I guide her to the bed, ease her down, and then rest my hand on her thigh. "You're beautiful, Joey. And you never have to hide from me. But...if you need to take a few minutes, or need to get dressed alone, or hell...

if you want to keep your shirt on during sex...all you have to do is tell me. I won't be angry, and it won't make me love you any less."

She wraps her arms around me, her face buried in the crook of my neck. She let me shower with her, and I thought... for a moment...she'd buried the last of her inhibitions. But I should have known better.

"You'll have good days and bad days, baby. We all do. Some nights, all I can see are the faces of the kids I lost right before I came back to San Diego. Others...it's the screams of my combat medic as a bomb took his leg. All I ask is that you don't shut me out. Tell me what you're feeling...when you can...and let me be there for you."

She starts to cry, tiny whimpers that break my heart. But after a few minutes, she sniffles and pulls back to wipe her cheeks with the backs of her hands. "I don't deserve you, Ford."

"Oh, yes you do. We were made for one another, Joey. And I'm going to spend the rest of my life proving it to you."

As I pour Joey her second cup of coffee, my doorbell rings. Joey tenses, but this is a safe neighborhood, and though Ronan went home a few hours ago, I don't expect trouble.

Until I see Ryker McCabe through the peephole, Wren tucked under his arm, and Dax standing at his side.

"Joey, come over here." There's no good reason for all three of them to show up at my front door together. Hell, the last I talked to Ryker, three days ago, he and Wren were still in Seattle.

"What is it?" She squeezes my hand so hard, I'm worried she'll dislocate one of my fingers, and I open the door, then curse to myself as Joey darts behind me. Ryker's a scary-looking dude under any circumstances, and Joey's still skittish.

Stepping back with Joey pressed against me, I gesture to my living room. "Didn't know we were hosting a party this morning. You couldn't have called first? Joey's—"

Wren steps forward and holds out her hand. "Joey? I'm Wren. It's really good to meet you."

Joey's trembling, but when I wrap my arm around her waist, she shakes Wren's hand. Her gaze darts between Ryker and Dax, and I make the introductions all around.

"Ford," Dax says, his slight Southern drawl a little more pronounced than usual. Tension lines bracket his lips, and his shoulders are hiked up close to his ears. "Can we sit down? Wren and Ryker found something on the surveillance tapes from Amir Faruk's compound."

Ryker stands behind Wren as she opens up her laptop and pulls up the video. Dax sits stiffly on one end of the couch, and Joey presses against me on the other. "This is from Nomar's bodycam," Wren says. "Before the three of you went in to rescue Joey."

We watch, and Joey turns her face against my shoulder as Faruk beats the crap out of her.

"Wren," I warn. "What's the point of this?"

"Sorry." Twin spots of color rise on her cheeks, and she skips ahead on the video. "Joey, you're off the video now. But you need to see this next part."

The man who helped us escape, the one who said he had to atone for his sins, trudges across the yard. Wren pauses the video, and Ryker clears his throat. "Do you know who that man is?"

"Isaad," Joey says quietly. "He was...kind."

I recount our escape and how Isaad directed us to the underground tunnel, and end with his final words to us. "He said Faruk took his name and his honor. Everything that made him who he...was. His ledger was full of blood. And if he was lucky, he'd be able to kill Faruk before Faruk killed him. And then he said he was sorry."

Ryker looks at Dax, then gives a little shake of his head. "That enough proof for you?"

"Yeah." He takes off his glasses and pinches the bridge of his nose. "I'm going with you, brother. At least to the safehouse in Kabul. If he's alive, I need to be there."

"Who?" I ask. "Who the hell is this Isaad guy? He didn't sound like a local."

Ryker pins me with a hard stare. "His name is Jackson Richards. But when we knew him, when he was the Communications Sergeant on our ODA team, we called him Ripper."

Dear Reader,

Thank you for reading BY LETHAL FORCE. This book was very special to me. Ford and Joey...they're older. So often, it's hard to find steamy romance novels with *mature* characters.

Because Ford and Joey are my age (give or take), I can relate to them. Just because someone's a little over forty, doesn't mean they can't still have an action-packed steamy life.

As you probably guessed from the ending of BY LETHAL FORCE, there's another book coming. And that book...well...it's going to be a doozy. RIPPER'S ALIVE!

FIGHTING FOR VALOR will be released on September 10, 2019. But you don't have to wait that long to find out what Ry, Dax, and the rest of Hidden Agenda get into next. Stay tuned for a short story from this crew sometime in July.

AND NOW...A little favor. I hope you'll take the time to review this book. Reviews can make a huge difference in whether a book is successful. They also make authors happy.

I couldn't do this job without you—the readers. I love each and every one of you, and I want to thank you one more time for reading BY LETHAL FORCE.

FROM PATRICIA

Over the past two years, the Away From Keyboard series has turned into something I could never have imagined.

These books let me work out some of my demons.

We all have them. Those emotional hangups that you don't want, but can't quite seem to escape? Maybe it's PTSD. Maybe it's anxiety. Depression. An injury. Maybe you're just having a really, really bad day/week/month/year.

When I finished Breaking His Code, I realized Cam and West had helped me. Every book since has helped even more.

I write these books so people like me can see that our flaws, our challenges, our hardships...they can be the things that also make us beautiful.

This book would not be what it is without the help and support of many people.

Annalise: my cheerleader, beta reader, and friend.

The Midnight Coven: I love you all, and I can't wait to see what we do together over the next year.

My Unstoppable Forces Reader Group: You all are excited with me, cheer me up when I'm down, and...you read my books. I mean...how cool is that?

And finally, Janie: You're like the cool kid in school I always wanted to be but wasn't. The one I never thought I'd actually be talking to on a regular basis because why would she ever notice me. Your books transport me whenever I pick one up, and your support means the world to me.

Love, Patricia

ABOUT THE AUTHOR

I've always made up stories. Sometimes I even acted them out. I probably shouldn't admit that my childhood best friend and I used to run around the backyard pretending to fly in our Invisible Jet and rescue Steve Trevor. Oops.

Now that I'm too old to spin around in circles with felt magic bracelets on my wrists, I put "pen to paper" instead. Figuratively, at least. Fingers to keyboard is more accurate.

Outside of my writing, I'm a professional editor, a software geek, a singer (in the shower only), and a runner. I love red wine, scotch (neat, please), and cider. Seattle is my home, and I share an old house with my husband and cats.

I'm on my fourth—fifth?—rewatching of the modern *Doctor Who*, and I think one particular quote from that show sums up my entire life.

"We're all stories, in the end. Make it a good one, eh?" — *The Eleventh Doctor, Doctor Who*

I hope your story is brilliant.

You can reach me all over the web...
patriciadeddy.com
patricia@patriciadeddy.com

facebook.com/patriciadeddyauthor

twitter.com/patriciadeddy

instagram.com/patriciadeddy

bookbub.com/profile/patricia-d-eddy

ALSO BY PATRICIA D. EDDY

Elemental Shifter

Hot werewolves and strong, powerful elementals. What's not to love?

A Shift in the Water

A Shift in the Air

By the Fates

Check out the By the Fates series if you love dark and steamy tales of witches, devils, and an epic battle between good and evil.

By the Fates, Freed

Destined: A By the Fates Story

By the Fates, Fought

By the Fates, Fulfilled

In Blood

If you love hot Italian vampires and and a human who can hold her own against beings far stronger, then the In Blood series is for you.

Secrets in Blood

Revelations in Blood

Contemporary and Erotic Romances

I don't just write paranormal. Whatever your flavor of romance, I've got you covered.

Holidays and Heroes

Beauty isn't only skin deep and not all scars heal. Come swoon over sexy vets and the men and women who love them.

Mistletoe and Mochas

Love and Libations

Away From Keyboard

Dive into a steamy mix of geekery and military might with the men and women of Emerald City Security and North-West Protective Services.

Breaking His Code

In Her Sights

On His Six

Second Sight

By Lethal Force

Restrained

Do you like to be tied up? Or read about characters who do? Enjoy a fresh BDSM series that will leave you begging for more.

In His Silks

Christmas Silks

All Tied Up For New Year's

In His Collar